Nothing But Love in Common

"I feel so good when I'm with you, Grady."

"That's promising." He grinned. "Especially since the feeling is mutual."

Lorna smiled warmly. "Yes, but doesn't it seem strange? We're so different from each other."

"Forget about our differences," he murmured tenderly. "They'll take care of themselves in time."

When he kissed her lips it was as though he were fulfilling some golden promise for which Lorna had waited all of her life. Her arms pulled him closer as she kissed him back with an intimacy that was all-consuming. She was lost in this spinning pleasure.

PENNY ALLISON
lives in Michigan with her husband of twenty years and their two children. A writer of nonfiction all her life, she says it was her favorite hobby, acting, that first led her to write romances. "I put myself into the characters as I write, and they just seem to come to life on their own."

Dear Reader:

I'd like to take this opportunity to thank you for all your support and encouragement of Silhouette Romances.

Many of you write in regularly, telling us what you like best about Silhouette, which authors are your favorites. This is a tremendous help to us as we strive to publish the best contemporary romances possible.

All the romances from Silhouette Books are for you, so enjoy this book and the many stories to come.

Karen Solem
Editor-in-Chief
Silhouette Books

PENNY ALLISON
Night Train to Paradise

Silhouette *Romance*

Published by Silhouette Books New York

America's Publisher of Contemporary Romance

Silhouette Books by Penny Allison

King of Diamonds (DES #20)
Reckless Venture (DES #65)
Night Train to Paradise (ROM #271)

SILHOUETTE BOOKS, a Division of Simon & Schuster, Inc.
1230 Avenue of the Americas, New York, N.Y. 10020

ISBN: 0-671-57271-7

First Silhouette Books printing January, 1984

10 9 8 7 6 5 4 3 2 1

Map by Ray Lundgren

SILHOUETTE, SILHOUETTE ROMANCE and colophon are
registered trademarks of Simon & Schuster, Inc.

America's Publisher of Contemporary Romance

Printed in the U.S.A.

To Anne Marie,
A Friend for All Seasons

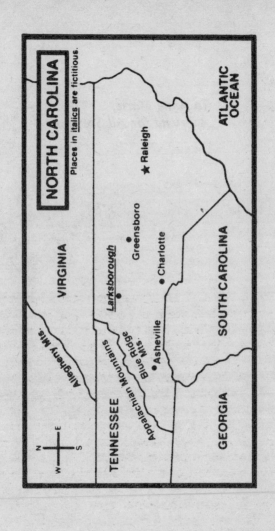

Chapter One

The jukebox played a bluegrass tune in her parents's roadside diner, as Lorna helped herself to coffee from behind the counter. It was an incongruous setting for her now. Six years had passed since the days when she had waited tables there. Today, she was a visitor, an elegantly turned out young woman in a designer suit of the palest gray, accented by the vibrant plum of a silk blouse and a matching pair of imported leather pumps. Her blonde hair, caught back in a tight chignon, bared her face starkly, but it was a look that she wore with aplomb. Even features and high cheekbones helped, of course, but Lorna had taken care to enhance them with a subtle blend of makeup. She knew how to apply foundation and blusher so that it illuminated her fair skin, while her blue eyes, due to her skill with liner and shadow, became two striking jewels on her face. Fashion was Lorna's livelihood, and she took it seriously. Had there really been a time when she wore a pink waitress's uniform and dime-store cosmetics? That dim memory of herself was like something from a different world.

She pushed her way carefully past the low, swinging doors at the counter, mindful of the steaming cup of coffee she held in her hand. Little enough had changed there since she had been away. The diner, enlivened with its usual soft-drink signs and a folksy hodgepodge of community notices, was deserted at that hour except for the familiar figure of her father, who sat half-hidden behind his newspaper for his midmorning coffee break. Lorna sat down across from him.

"Anything new and interesting in the world, daddy?" she asked brightly, hoping to engage him in some kind of conversation. She knew it wouldn't be easy. After six years up North, she seemed to have become a virtual stranger to her family. Even her speech was no longer the same as theirs, and in her voice there lingered only the softest traces of a native North Carolina drawl.

"Looks like the Rebels should have a pretty good season, according to what Grady McGraw has to say," her father mumbled from behind the pages of the *Larksborough Courier*, too absorbed in his article to leave it for the moment.

Lorna frowned, trying to place the name of Grady McGraw. It sounded vaguely familiar; he was some sort of sports figure, she seemed to recall, although which sport he was in she couldn't be sure. "Oh, don't you mean the bas-

ketball coach at Southern Tech?" she asked her
father in an earnest attempt at conversation.

A wry chuckle was heard from behind the
paper. "Football coach, sugar, football. It's up to
McGraw to see that the Rebels kick the ball, not
shoot it into a basket. You've been away so long,
Lorna Lee, that I believe you've forgotten everything."

Then she was laughing in protest as she
punched the paper playfully. "Put that thing
away, daddy, and please be fair. You know that I
never followed sports, not even before I went
away."

"Well, that's a fact." The paper was lowered to
reveal the droll, happy-go-lucky countenance of
Mack Lambert, who, with his wife, ran Mack and
Annie's Diner with the easy informality of a
picnic on a back porch. Lorna's parents had never
made much money with their brand of business
management, but they remained blithely unper-
turbed by it. It wasn't as if they couldn't try to
improve their situation, Lorna thought fretfully.
If they simply put up a sign on the main highway,
they might get more customers. Although they
had talked of it for years, it was one of those
things that they "just never got around to doing."
Lorna sighed under her breath as she met her
father's eyes. As a part-time fiddler of country
music, it often seemed to her that he had chosen
to fiddle his life away. He was a dear man, but
how exasperating, too! The feeling, though,
seemed to be mutual.

"My goodness, is that you, Lorna Lee!" he
exclaimed at the sight of his daughter's picture-

perfect elegance. "Sometimes I can't hardly believe that such a fashionable lady is my own flesh-and-blood!"

"Oh, I am. You know that I am." Impulsively, Lorna reached for his bony hand, squeezing it as much to convince him as herself. While she knew that he was secretly proud that she had put herself through college—the only one of his children to do so—Lorna knew, too, that it had created a gap between them, one that seemed to grow wider with each passing day. "I can be both your daughter and a 'fashionable lady,' too," she explained, using his quaint phrase in an attempt to meet him on his own ground. "Besides, I want to make a nice impression. I've got that interview for the fashion writer's job at the *Courier* today, remember?"

"Except that I have to keep pinching myself to believe it, girl. I thought you'd never come back to this place after all those years in Chicago."

Actually, Lorna had thought so, too. When she left Larksborough behind at the age of eighteen, she was fully convinced that she would never return. There she was, though, in hopes of putting her education to good use. Ironically enough, jobs were scarcer in the industrial North than in the South at that time; poor economic conditions, in fact, had forced the department store in Chicago where Lorna had worked as a fashion consultant to close its doors for good. But her homecoming was not one she viewed as a personal defeat. Far from it. She had come a long way for herself over the years. Once a naive country girl, she had become a knowledgeable woman, sophisticated, too, thanks entirely to her own determination to create a better life for herself than she had known in childhood.

"Well, if those folks at the paper have any sense, they'll give you the job right off the bat," her father was saying. "Anyone can see that you know everything there is to know about wearing the right kind of clothes."

"Thanks, daddy." Lorna's smile masked an underlying sense of sadness, for she was struck again by how little he really knew about what her work involved. But a quick glance at her watch told her that she had no time for further explanation. She rose to plant a kiss on top of his balding head. "Will you wish me luck? I've got to be getting on my way."

He nodded slowly. "You're always on your way, sugar, and I've never tried to stop you. Of course, you're not going far this time, and that's a comfort. If you do get the job, you can always stay here with your mama and me. That old room is yours, you know, if you still want it."

"But we've been through that before," Lorna said as gently as she could. She had grown far too independent to live with her parents, a natural-enough state of affairs that they could not seem to understand.

Thankfully, though, Mack Lambert chose not to dwell on this awkward issue; instead, he changed the subject. "Well, maybe you'll run into McGraw down there at the paper—he writes a football column once a week." A boyish twinkle lit up her father's eyes at the thought of his favorite sport. "And if he isn't too busy coaching the Rebels, you tell him to get on over here for our Friday night special—all the fried chicken he can eat at the best prices around!"

"Just let me get the job first." Lorna giggled. "Then I'll see what I can do." It was crazy to think of inviting such a person—what was his name again?—to Mack and Annie's Diner, which was frequented largely by truckers and millworkers. Her eyes fell to the newspaper to check the man's by-line. Well, even if this Grady McGraw person liked southern fried chicken, she strongly doubted that he would choose to eat it there.

Then she was off, the screen door banging behind her as she stepped onto the front porch. "Move, Rasmus," she ordered the indolent hound who lay before her. He obeyed with a reluctant sigh and a doleful look of his brown eyes.

Looking about at the unchanged setting as she walked to her car, Lorna was greeted by a rush of memories, not all of them entirely pleasant. The diner itself, tucked into a grove of cypress trees, was the same as ever, a modest, log-cabin-styled structure, just barely on the right side of being seedy. If anything, Lorna supposed, it had a homespun sort of charm, enhanced by a hand-lettered sign in the window: "There are no strangers here—only friends we've never met before." That sign had been a part of Lorna's childhood, along with notices of special prices on the dishes that her mother prepared in the kitchen. "Sweet potato pie—whole or by the slice" and "Hush puppies made daily—best you've ever tried."

Since the Lambert family home lay directly behind their place of business, Lorna had, to all intents and purposes, grown up inside the diner, playing there when she was little and waiting tables as she grew older. Not for her an ordinary house where she could bring her friends but this ramshackle building instead. Well, the days when she had been teased by her schoolmates—"Mack and Annie's daughter; fetch me a glass of water!" —were long since gone. She wasn't the same person anymore; such memories, in fact, shouldn't have the power to upset her at all. Lorna bit her lip as she waited for her car to start, the engine turning over with some reluctance on the second try. If the truth were known, Mack and Annie's Diner was still an embarrassment to her. As much as she hated to admit it, there was no escaping that sad fact. And Mack and Annie themselves, her very own parents, affected her in much the same way. She loved them dearly, but why, oh, why, couldn't they change with the times, if only just a little?

Nevertheless, her short drive into Larksborough was pleasant, marked by rolling hills and dense thickets of tall pines. Yes, she was home again, not deeply regretting it after the gray, impersonal streets of Chicago. Besides, her interview, whether successful or not, certainly promised to be interesting, because it was Roger Haskell himself with whom she would be meeting!

She slowed down a little as she passed Calhoun High where she had first seen Roger. The building looked smaller, far less imposing than she remembered it. Lorna smiled, knowing that Roger, too, might appear equally diminished by time. Teenage idols had a way of fading, especially when they were no longer viewed through star-struck adolescent eyes.

Lorna drove on. Thankfully, Roger had no way of knowing how important he had once been in her life. Two years ahead of her and the son of the wealthy owner of the *Larksborough Courier*, he had never known that Lorna Lee Lambert existed. Roger Haskell had moved in privileged circles, drawing his friends from the select country-club set, all of whom reigned supreme within the walls of class-conscious Calhoun High. As a result, Lorna had worshiped Roger from afar as though he were a star in a distant galaxy. Handsome, blond and always dressed with an aura that suggested old money and good breeding, Roger had been, to Mack and Annie's daughter, the epitome of everything that seemed worth having. Surely, he would be the perfect escort, and Lorna had pictured herself on his arm, equaling the elegance of his wardrobe in a swirling prom dress of white chiffon. That had never happened. In her discount-store dresses, she had been virtually invisible to someone in Roger's position. He had graduated, in fact, without once looking her way. How was he to know that such aloof behavior, as much as anything else in the world, would serve as the motivation that caused Lorna Lambert to change her life so completely?

Before she knew it, though, she found herself pulling into the parking lot of the *Courier* where Roger now served as the managing editor. Lorna parked her car and then checked her reflection in

the rear-view mirror. Even the heat of this southern September day had done nothing to alter her
immaculate grooming. In fact, she very much
resembled that long-ago fantasy of herself as the
girl on Roger Haskell's arm. Her memory of him,
though, was not clear at all, having faded over the
years into a blurred and foggy image. Lorna
smiled softly as she wondered how her former
teenage idol would look to her now. If nothing
else, she thought, her interview would certainly
be an interesting one!

But she discovered, to her chagrin, that it had
been postponed with no notice at all. "Mr.
Haskell is not available today," snapped his receptionist, a bespectacled lady of cold efficiency
who sat like a watchdog in the quiet plushness of
the executive area. "He's been called away on a
labor dispute, and under the circumstances, his
absence was unavoidable." Then she surveyed
Lorna's appearance with a grudging look of respect. "I'm sure that he'll still want to meet with
you, Miss Lambert, so I'll schedule you for another day. I hope Monday morning will be convenient."

Since the woman's pencil was poised and ready
just above a blank line in her appointment book,
Lorna merely nodded. Surely, she could have
been notified of this change in plans by telephone!
That would have been the courteous thing to do,
but instead of saying this to the receptionist, she
decided to bite her tongue. There was no sense in
starting off on the wrong foot. First impressions
were important, and maybe both Roger and his
grim-faced receptionist had been too busy to call.

At any rate, Lorna was in no position to alienate them. After agreeing to the Monday appointment with a pleasant smile thrown in for good measure, Lorna turned to leave. Still, she was annoyed and badly disappointed. There she was, on her way back to the parking lot, all dressed up with no one to see!

Outside, the noonday sun was high in the sky, while from the grassy field behind the parking lot Lorna heard a noisy group of men engaged in a boisterous game of touch football. Her eyes wandered in their direction without any great interest. They were probably workman from the adjacent print shop of the *Courier* who were on their lunch hour, marking the arrival of the college football season at nearby Southern Tech with this skirmish of their own. Lorna watched them charge at each other, wondering what it was about the game that held such appeal for her father and every other member of the male sex in town as well. In her eyes it had never been anything but an unappealing tangle in which burly men knocked each other to the ground for no reason that she had ever been able to discern. The ball spun dizzily through the air, while from atop a picnic table, a lone workman, in a grubby pair of overalls, was loudly shouting encouragement to his friends as he unpeeled a snack-time banana.

When his eyes fell upon Lorna, however, he did a sudden double take. "Hey take a look at what's coming our way! Ain't she a fine and fancy sight to see!"

All at once, the warm air resounded with

whistles and catcalls as the players stopped their game to watch Lorna walk by. She turned her head away, pretending not to see or hear them. Nevertheless, their voices reached her ears with piercing clarity. "Fine as wine in the summertime!" and "Come on over here, pretty mama. I want to talk to you!"

Oh, this was embarrassing; even worse was that she was still a long way from her car. She continued to hold her head up, though, even as she hastened her steps. She might have missed inspection that day from Roger Haskell, she thought wryly, but she certainly hadn't missed it from these unruly characters!

At last, she slipped gratefully into the privacy of her car, aware that their eyes were still following her. Well, soon enough they wouldn't have anything more to look at, she thought as she quickly placed the key in the ignition. Never had the engine taken so long to turn over. Of course, it had acted strangely earlier that day, but even so, it had started. This time, though, after the third try, Lorna had the sinking feeling that it wasn't going to start. Besides, if she kept on trying, she knew that she would flood it. Now what? she asked herself in silent frustration. She would have to call a service station, which would take both time and money, more than she could easily afford to part with at the moment. What a day this had been! She probably should have avoided it altogether by simply staying in bed.

Adding to her troubles was that the workmen were still eying her. One of them, in fact, the biggest of the lot, with a crown of rust-colored hair that stood out vibrantly in the distance, seemed intent on coming her way.

"Time out!" he called to his companions as he deftly hurled the football into a whirling arc against the wide blue sky. Then he was jogging swiftly in Lorna's direction, while the others observed him with gleeful hoots of laughter.

"Score one for me, old buddy!"

"Look at that man go! He's on the right track, but that's why they call him 'Night Train'!"

Lorna watched him approach, feeling like a sitting duck. The last thing she needed was a head-on collision with a man called Night Train, but as he came toward her, his big body charged with a sense of overpowering strength and energy, she sensed that such a collision could not be avoided.

All too soon he was at her side, leaning down to meet her eyes. "Don't listen to them," he said of his raucous companions. "They do call me Night Train, but only because I've been known to rush to the rescue. I can see that you're in trouble, and I'd like to help you out."

In contrast to the others, he seemed courteous enough, even surprisingly gentle in the manner of many a big, physical man when in the presence of a woman. Then, too, he had the most remarkable face that Lorna had ever seen. Not handsome—his features were far too rugged and craggy for that—but they were marked by a strength of character, a certain kind of rough-hewn majesty that seemed to have been carved from granite itself. And underneath his thatch of tousled hair, burnished in the sun, she saw a pair of blue-green eyes, twinkling at her vividly and filled with genuine sparks of kindness.

"Thank you," she told him a little shyly. "I thought I'd call a service station. You really don't have to trouble yourself."

At this, he grinned warmly, as crinkly laugh lines played about his eyes. He probably laughed often, Lorna thought. It looked as if he lived life as it came, meeting it with a full store of easy good humor. "Look, I'm right here, and you won't have to wait for service from me. My prices are good, too. All I ask is a smile, nothing more than that. I promise."

"Well," she replied, weakening, "I'm not sure if—"

He patted the hood of her car. "Let me have a look inside. But first I want to see you smile. I'm not as bad as I might look," he added as he dismissed his outfit—a brown sweatshirt and a rumpled pair of khakis—with bemusement. "I wasn't born beautiful, but you can't hold that against me. And I'm entirely respectable. I even pay my bills on time."

Suddenly, Lorna found herself laughing, her head thrown back in a spontaneous burst of merriment. Her day had gone badly so far, but it wasn't hopeless. Not while the sun shone so brightly overhead and someone with the outrageous name of Night Train was offering his help with such funny, down-to-earth generosity.

"Much better," he said in glad appreciation of her laughter. "In fact, I'll count it as payment in full. I couldn't ask for anything nicer than that."

Lorna released the lever to the hood, her face still wreathed in smiles. The man did seem respectable enough in a down-to-earth way. Besides, he possessed such an air of easygoing competence that it seemed foolish to refuse his offer of help. Soon she was standing beside him as he checked the engine, wondering what she could do to assist him.

He was, however, completely self-sufficient as he began to examine the complex network of pipes, tubes and wiring that comprised the inner workings of her car. Lorna watched him gravely. This was serious business, of course, made all the more complicated by the fact that she knew precious little about any kind of machinery. It was a mystery to her, but he approached it with the ready skill of a mechanic.

"Your wires are tight," he observed at last.

Since there was a smile on his face as he spoke, Lorna could only suppose that this meant good news. "That's all right, though, isn't it?" she asked, just to make sure.

"It's fine. Those sparks won't ignite without a tight connection. But that's not your problem. We'll just have to keep on trouble-shooting until we find out what it is."

Lorna was aware that he had begun to appraise her slowly, his eyes traveling from her face to her figure and right down to the shape of her well-formed legs. It was a look of frank masculine appreciation, but nonetheless there was nothing leering about it. If anything, it held a promise of warm friendliness, as though he sought to know her better. But the small warning that sounded in her mind caused Lorna to turn away. She knew virtually nothing about this man—only that he was evidently a workman from the print shop of the paper where she hoped to be hired as a fashion writer. It was obvious that they inhabited two separate worlds; in fact, he seemed to recognize it, too.

"I mostly work outdoors, so I don't get a chance to see many people who look like you. Don't tell me now. You must be a fashion model."

"Well, not exactly," Lorna replied, not wanting to divulge too much information. Still, he seemed sincerely interested, and the urge to confide in him was too tempting to ignore. "But I did want to make a good impression. You see, I applied for a new job today."

"Did you get it?" His tone was pleasant and conversational as he fell to his work again.

Lorna frowned, remembering how her interview with Roger Haskell had been postponed. "I don't know yet. I should find out on Monday."

"My guess is that you will—get the job, that is," her companion replied as he turned to look at her with an optimistic smile. "Anyway, I hope so. I'd like to be a friend of yours."

Underneath the sun, his hair burned reddish gold, while his dancing eyes held an invitation too candid and too direct to possibly ignore. Lorna felt something warm within her, and for a moment she smiled back at him. But only for a moment. This encounter in the parking lot wasn't going as it should. There was a definite current in the air, and she knew that she must try to discourage this man tactfully, just as she had done with that young delivery boy in Chicago when he had grown overly friendly at work. There was a fine line that must be drawn in these kinds of situations, especially when they cut across the boundaries that were supposed to separate blue-collar people from professionals.

Thankfully, though, her companion turned back to her car. It was when he unfastened a black plastic cap for inspection that he let out a long, low whistle. "You know, for a lady who looks like she stepped right out of a bandbox, you really do surprise me. You've been driving around with one mighty greasy distributor cap, did you know that?"

Lorna couldn't help but laugh again, wishing that this man didn't have the ability to infuse her with such a lighthearted spirit. No, she hadn't realized that the distributor cap was greasy; even if she had, though, she wouldn't have known that it mattered. It evidently did, however; enough so that it prevented her car from starting.

The problem was solved by a good, brisk cleaning that her companion performed with the aid of a rag that Lorna had found in her glove compartment. "I don't think you'd ever forget to shine those nice new shoes of yours," he counseled her in a teasing way. "Just remember to do the same every once in a while for the parts of your car. It'll drive better for you if you do. Safer, too. You've got to promise to take care of these things. I'd hate to lose you to a greasy distributor cap out there on the highway."

Lorna bit her lip to keep from smiling at him again. There was nothing funny about the situation, but there was something in this man's charming way of handling it that made her feel warm inside and delightfully feminine, too. Of course, that was only because he was such a contrast to her—a powerfully built man who plainly lived a life of strenuous physical activity. He moved easily within his big body, as though it had served him well, while his clothing was just a covering of the most functional kind. Suitable enough, Lorna concluded, for the kind of job he must have and a reminder, too, that the other men from the print shop had already returned to their shift.

"Shouldn't you be getting back to work?" she asked him nervously. "You don't have to be late on my account."

At this, he threw back his head and laughed heartily. "Don't worry about me. I make my own hours—it's the only way to work." Then he shut the hood of her car with confidence. "It should start for you now. Why don't you give it a try?"

Soon Lorna's ears were rewarded with the healthy sounds of a purring engine while she smiled brightly at Night Train from the driver's seat. "Thank you so much for all of your help. It was more than kind of you to take so much trouble and—"

"No trouble," he reassured her as he cocked his head in the direction of the engine. Then he began resting his bare forearms on her open window as if he had the rest of the day to talk to her. "Those sparks are really flying now, wouldn't you say?"

"Uh, yes, they are . . ." She felt herself blush as her voice trailed off, too embarrassed by his obvious double meaning to continue.

This only encouraged him further. "What did you say your name was again?" he asked with a charming smile.

She hadn't mentioned it, of course, but now she supposed that she must make some response. Still, she turned from the lively interest she read in his eyes, averting her glance to his arms, instead—rock hard and glistening with burnished hairs under the midday sun. "I'm—I'm Miss Lambert," she told him, hating the stiff way it sounded but certain, too, that it was time for her to draw the line.

He chuckled incredulously. "There must be more to it than that. Look, since we're going to be friends, we should know each other's names."

"But we already do," she protested in a light, firm tone of voice. "I'm Miss Lambert, and you're—you're Mr. Night Train." A crazy giggle escaped from her throat before she could conclude on a more serious note. "I hope you don't mind if I call you that. It does seem to suit you, just like Miss—Miss Lambert suits me, too, under the circumstances."

He nodded slowly and with a philosophical air of good humor. "Oh, I get it," he teased. "You're making sure that I know you're a lady, a touch-me-not lady, at that." Then he surveyed his big hands, grimy from the repair work on her car, with a lopsided grin that was fully disarming. "I don't suppose this old grease devil can even expect a handshake from a fine lady like you."

All at once, Lorna found herself reaching for his hand, not caring at all that it was dirty. She wanted only to thank him for his generous help. She was not prepared, though, for the response that flooded her at the clasp of his hand, nor did she expect to feel just what she did from a simple handshake. There was strength in his touch, firm and filled with a sure sense of forceful energy. But there was goodness in it, too, as fundamental and as radiant as the life-giving sun that shone over-head. For the moment, she was aware of nothing but his hand enclosing hers and an all-pervasive sense of warmth.

Then she pulled back, unnerved and shaken. Surely, she had been detained there long enough and should be getting on her way. Still, he delayed her departure with a brief question, uttered gently and with a coaxing lilt of his voice.

"Friends, Miss Lambert?"

"Friends, Mr. Night Train," she heard herself reply. It was the only response she could give, for it was then that his keen eyes seemed to probe beneath her polished surface to touch the woman who lived within.

But what was wrong with her, anyway, she thought as she drove away. She must put him out of her mind, of course, especially if she was hired by Roger Haskell as the *Courier*'s new fashion writer. Any involvement with a workman from the Haskells' print shop was sure to get her off to a poor start. Then, too, Roger was having labor problems, caused, for all Lorna knew, by Night Train himself, who made his own hours at the *Courier's* expense. Yes, he possessed a diamond-in-the-rough sort of appeal, but what of it? Besides, why should he have affected her? For a long time, she had kept a picture in her mind of the type of man who would be right for her. Such an image, in fact, had been inspired originally by Roger Haskell, with whom she would be meeting on Monday. If she had to think of anyone, then surely it should be of him, not of some man called by the unlikely name of Night Train whom she had met in the *Courier's* parking lot! She could not afford to give him a second thought.

It wasn't until that night that she allowed herself to think of him again. Nestled in bed in the small room that had been hers in childhood, Lorna was aware of the faint sounds of a train as it rumbled along the tracks that lay in the distance. It was a haunting sound, musical, too, and its whistle drifted like a muffled song to her ears. When she was a child, she had envisioned herself traveling on that train, wishing that it could carry her to some mysterious, far-flung destination that she had never known before. She wished the same thing now; only her drowsy thoughts reminded her that somewhere out there lived a man named Night Train whose hair seemed to catch fire under the shining rays of the sun. To allow herself another picture of him was a foolish indulgence, but it was one that she was far too sleepy to resist. Lorna closed her eyes, letting her thoughts take her where they would. When she succumbed to sleep at last, there was a faint smile on her face.

Chapter Two

Lorna returned to the *Courier* for her interview on Monday morning, half hoping to see a burly, redheaded man hailing her from the parking lot. She didn't, though; at this hour of the day, there were no signs of life outside the building. It was a good thing, too, that she didn't spot Night Train, Lorna reminded herself as she tucked the ends of her new paisley scarf beneath the lapels of her suit jacket. Her meeting with Roger Haskell was just minutes away. The last thing she needed was to be detained by one of his workmen in a repeat performance of Friday's lively encounter.

She breathed deeply, trying to calm her nerves as she walked inside the building. She had a lot at stake today—the chance of getting a good new job, of course, as well as the chance to satisfy her curiosity about Roger Haskell. What had he become in all these years? Had he changed as much as she, and if so, how? She wondered. Yes, she wanted the job, but she also wanted very much to know how Roger, whom she had once idolized, would affect the woman she was today.

Twenty minutes later, as Lorna sat stiffly in the pompous presence of the paper's managing editor, she wondered what it was about him that had ever intrigued her. Yes, he was good-looking, but no more so than many other men. Besides, his behavior—in this businesslike setting, at least— was so coldly impersonal that it bordered on rudeness. He had not once apologized for failing to keep his original appointment with her, and his reaction upon learning that she had grown up in the southeast section of Larksborough had been subtly condescending. "It's no wonder that I don't remember you," he told her dryly. "I never managed to get into that part of town."

Of course, he had shown signs of snobbishness in high school, but if such behavior had seemed appropriate then, it did not seem so now. They were no longer students who were locked into the rigid caste system at Calhoun High; if anything, Lorna thought, they had become equals in education and in other ways, too. Besides, why should he care what part of town she used to live in? She had outgrown it long before; in any case, she certainly wasn't planning a permanent retreat back to the world of Mack and Annie's Diner.

Still, she did not wish to judge him unfairly. She wanted, in fact, to be able to like him, if only for the sake of old times and nostalgia. Of course, he was young, she reasoned, and since he had just stepped into his father's shoes at the *Courier,* it was possible that he was covering up a newcomer's lack of confidence. Then, too, he still knew how to dress. Lorna had to give him credit for that. His three-piece gray suit, cut from the finest of flannel, was just the right outfit for a rising young executive in his position, while his pale blond hair had been styled and blow-dried with real expertise. In fact, Roger Haskell, with his obvious taste in dress and grooming, looked in every way like the type of man Lorna preferred to date. If only he didn't appear, at the same time, to be such a stuffed shirt!

He cleared his throat, finally looking up from her résumé for the first time during the interview. "Well," he pronounced in his loftiest tones, "you seem to meet most of my requirements, especially in contrast to some of the other examples of local talent that I've seen around here." A flicker of disdain crossed his face before he continued. "It's my belief that the *Courier* badly needs a new image, a kind of face lift, as it were, and a qualified fashion writer might be useful for that reason. I'd be willing to try you out—that is, of course, if you are interested in the position."

"Yes, I am interested," Lorna replied, her voice sounding thin and uncertain. She tried again. "I'd be glad to accept the job, and I assure you that I'll do my very best," she added on a more positive note. In many ways, it was a good job, and she wished she could feel happier that she had gotten it.

A ritualized handshake, as barren of genuine

feeling as the interview itself, followed. Surely, there must be something behind Roger's icy façade of executive efficiency, but if so, Lorna detected no positive vibrations. She knew only that the touch of his well-manicured hand was chilly in hers, offering nothing of himself at all. How different, she recalled for a fleeting moment, from the red-headed man whose touch had flooded her with such dazzling warmth. But what an absurd comparison, she told herself sharply. Roger Haskell, newly appointed to the top position of authority at the *Courier,* could not afford personal involvement with a new and untested employee, while her friend from the parking lot plainly had little to lose.

Nevertheless, Lorna left Roger's presence with a sense of real relief. Job interviews weren't supposed to be fun, but her new boss had shown as much personal charm as a frozen fish. Although it was possible, she supposed, that he might thaw in time. Besides, she had a new job to occupy her mind, and there were certainly other men in the world besides Roger. But now that she was back in Larksborough, North Carolina, she reminded herself wryly, where would she ever meet one who could live up to all of her high standards?

She pushed the thought from her mind as she walked quickly through the building, anxious to be outside. The artificial lighting above made a poor substitute for the Indian summer sun that she knew was shining in the sky. Soon she reached a corridor that led to the parking lot. She rounded it sharply, her vision obscured by the foliage of an enormous potted tree that marked off the executive area from the other offices. And suddenly she found herself up against a moving mass that had been heading in her direction. At eye level, she saw only a broad expanse of navy blue, but above that snapped a vivid pair of blue-green eyes and an unruly head of flame-colored hair that could belong to only one person at the *Larksborough Courier.*

"Oh!" she exclaimed breathlessly, stepping back from the solid impact of his hard, muscular body so close against her own. "I didn't know it was you. Don't you ever look where you're going, Mr. Night Train?"

"Always, Miss Lambert," he reassured her with a pleased ripple of laughter. "You don't, though. The way you came charging at me I thought maybe you'd just seen a ghost. If that's the case, then I really won't hold it against you."

To him, it was obviously just an amusing joke, but Lorna still felt badly shaken. Besides, what was he doing there, so far from the print shop? "Don't be silly," she told him a little more crossly than she had intended as she began to smooth her suit jacket into place. "I was just coming from Mr. Haskell's office and—"

At this, he chuckled heartily, the bold contours of his face flexing easily into an expression of ready humor. "Then you did see a ghost," he said teasingly. "Or at least the closest thing we have to one around here. Roger can be enough to give anyone the chills. I was just on my way to see him myself, so I know how you must feel. That's the way he is, though, so you shouldn't let it get you down." Then he shifted the stance of his tall body and folded his arms casually against the breadth of his chest. "But tell me about you. I seem to recall that you were applying for a job today. I'll bet you got it, too."

Lorna couldn't help but brighten at his warm interest. After all, she had good news to tell, and it would be pleasant to share it with someone who was so clearly receptive. "Well, yes, I did," she admitted proudly. "I'll be starting next week!"

"What did I tell you?" said her companion, rewarding her with a congratulatory grin that spread from ear to ear. "I thought you would. And just in case Roger didn't mention it, let me say 'welcome aboard' for the rest of us. What kind of job did you get for yourself, anyway?"

In his presence, Lorna found herself laughing spontaneously once more, but it seemed the only possible reaction to his friendly, easygoing air of optimism. He had no way of knowing that she would get the job because he didn't even know what kind of work she did. Still, it was a pleasure to receive such a well-meant vote of confidence, and how nice to know that somebody cared! "I was hired as a fashion writer," she finally explained, smiling.

At this, she saw a streak of mischief cross his face, the perfect compliment to his thick, tousled mane of rust-colored hair. "I might have known." He chuckled. "Well, you should do very well at that. Just remember to take pity on the rest of us, though. We can't all look like you do. In fact, some of us are just about hopeless when it comes to fashion."

He was probably referring to himself, Lorna surmised, watching him casually pull his sweat-shirt down over his belt. His khaki pants were as rumpled as they had been on Friday, while his boots looked well worn, as though he had come inside from tramping around a muddy field. No, he hardly represented a picture of the latest fashion; nevertheless, Lorna could tell that he possessed every possibility for real improvement. Even now he cut a fine figure for himself, but what a well-tailored suit wouldn't do for those powerful shoulders and for the forthright stance of those long, lean legs! He could look truly distinguished once his rough edges were smoothed over by the right kinds of clothes. At any rate, he certainly could use some guidelines for the way to look when meeting with his boss.

"Well, the point of my job will be to help people look just as good as they can," she ex-plained earnestly, trying to dispel the note of amusement that she read in his twinkling eyes. "Since appearances are so important, especially in the work place, we can all benefit by—"

"Wait a minute," he interrupted her with a sly chuckle. "Don't tell me that you'll be running around here in white gloves and making sure that everyone else is wearing them, too."

"No, of course not," she told him, growing a little annoyed. This, after all, was her new job that they were discussing, and if he thought it silly and inconsequential, she most certainly did not. "But I will be giving advice and information to people who want it. You see, my background is in fashion and design, and I happen to take it seriously. Besides, it's been shown that the right kind of wardrobe is a real asset to people who want to move ahead in their jobs. It does take a certain amount of planning and coordination, but—"

"Slow down, Miss Lambert," put in her companion in a playful tone of voice. "I think I detect a trace of missionary zeal in your manner, so maybe I should stay clear of your path. At any rate, I'm one man you'll never convert to the cause."

"And why not?" Lorna asked him sternly. "It could make a difference to you. You might not like Mr. Haskell, for instance, but he is in charge here. And you're going in to see him looking like you just pulled away from a football game in the parking lot. That's not the best way to make a good impression, you know, especially on your boss."

Those were strong words, stronger even than Lorna had intended. But she meant what she said. It was through fashion that she had made a better life for herself, and she was anxious to show others that it could help them, too. She saw, however, that her words had made no impact. To her total chagrin, the big man before her simply threw back his head and laughed with relish. "I'm not worried," he said at last. "The fact of the matter is that Roger has to take me any way that he can get me. I do my job, and he can't seem to find anyone who can take my place."

The impudence of the man! It was no wonder

that Roger was having labor problems, thought Lorna in his defense. Evidently, he had his hands full if the attitude of Night Train was typical. And perhaps it was. It seemed entirely plausible that he was acting as the spokesman for the others and that he was about to visit Roger's office with a long list of impossible demands. One of them was probably the right to look as gloriously unkempt as possible; another, no doubt, was the right to keep free and easy hours in the print shop!

Lorna sighed. She knew little enough about this man except that he needed to be taken down a peg or two. Thankfully, though, that was a job for Roger and not for her. "Well, I won't keep you from your meeting with Mr. Haskell," she told him coolly. "Anyway, I have to be leaving now."

"But you're leaving in a tiff, and I don't want you to do that." Suddenly, his voice grew low, beguilingly gentle, before he placed one of his big hands with tender persuasion on her shoulder. "Look, we may not see eye to eye on fashion, but that doesn't have to stand in our way. A little healthy difference of opinion makes things lively. And interesting, too. Always interesting." He smiled coaxingly, his eyes engaging her with such warmth that she could not turn away. It was crazy, of course, to allow him to stand so close, but the vital presence of his powerful body held a fascination all its own. She was aware of his scent, faintly musky and hinting of the pine-filled breezes that came from outdoors. "Come on now," he continued very softly. "You know that I was teasing you, don't you? Just try not to take things so seriously, including your new job. It's better to laugh than to frown, and it's much nicer to be friends than enemies. I can't let you go away angry."

"I'm not exactly angry," Lorna tried to explain, although she was, just a little. "It's just that— well, I simply can't agree with your attitude."

"You don't have to agree with it. All you have to do is to accept me for what I am, and I'll accept you, too. It's a matter of live and let live. How about it, Miss Lambert? Can we reach a settlement?"

He was smiling, although Lorna could tell that he spoke from deep conviction, as though his words represented a code of staunchly held beliefs from which he could never be shaken. A stubborn man, perhaps, who seemed in every way her direct opposite, but in spite of that, there was an undeniable current of feeling between them, a spontaneous rapport that sprang to life in each other's company. "Yes, I think we can reach a settlement," she heard herself say softly. "If you keep your end of the bargain, then I'll keep mine, too."

"It's a deal," he told her with an engaging grin, "as long as we can still be friends."

Lorna laughed, much too readily, she thought, before she began to back away from him. She was in no position to stand there talking to him all day long; it was high time to cut things short. "Oh, by all means, Mr. Night Train," she replied as she continued to put a distance between them. "But even friends have to go their separate ways. So I'll say good-by for now and let you get on with your meeting in Mr. Haskell's office. I'm sure you'll stand your ground with him quite well."

Then she turned face forward to walk briskly down the hallway, aware that his eyes were following her as she stepped along in her high-heeled pumps. Well, what of it, she thought lightly. The line between them had been marked clearly, and if he wished to continue teasing her, then she didn't really mind. Although she hadn't started her job yet, she had, it seemed, already made a friend at work, someone who would greet her with a smile in the mornings and who could be counted on to make her laugh when she left the parking lot at night. It would all be harmless enough—she would certainly see to that—but in the meantime, she felt an unreasonable ray of happiness shine through her. Letting herself out of the building, she was met by an azure sky and the fresh scent of Carolina pines that drifted down from distant hills.

Chapter Three

Lorna had the uneasy feeling that her coworkers did not know what to make of her. Of course, the paper had never hired anyone to write exclusively about fashion before; the position, in fact, had been Roger Haskell's idea, and the other staff reporters, most of them old-timers whose careers had been spent entirely within the traditions of small-town journalism, were not taking kindly to their young boss's plans for a "face lift." Well, they would get used to them gradually, Lorna kept reminding herself, just as they would get used to her, too. In her elegant outfits, each of them chosen with her cultivated flare for style and design, she did not look like the others, but surely that was as things had to be. She had a certain image to maintain if she wished to be taken seriously as a fashion authority. She had, after all, been hired for that purpose, and since her new boss wanted to bring greater sophistication to the paper, it was her job to work toward that goal.

Still, it felt uncomfortable to be so set apart from the others. They viewed her with guarded suspicion, almost as though she were a strange alien from another planet. Roger remained aloof, and he was giving her no support, while she found herself generally left out of the round of good-natured joking and gossip that went on between the other staff reporters. In fact, Lorna began to hope wistfully for a few more chance encounters with Night Train. At least his was a friendly face, but although she kept an eye out for him, she saw no signs of him at all during her first few weeks on the job.

Not that she was going to make a fool of herself by inquiring of the other men from the print shop as to his whereabouts. They were as raucous as ever, causing Lorna to avoid them as best she could. Just the day before, in fact, one of them had hailed her loudly in the parking lot with a clownish invitation to go dancing, only to be interrupted by a grinning companion. "That lady won't look your way, boy! She's waitin' for the night train to come along!" No, as pleasant as it might be to see him again, Lorna definitely could not afford to ask where he was.

Her only real companion at the *Courier* seemed to be Billy Ray Turner, a wily old reporter who had covered, in his time, "everything from circuses to city council meetings—not that there's much difference between the two," he confessed to Lorna with a gleeful chuckle. Now, in fact, he was lounging against her desk, having just finished his morning cup of coffee.

"How about if we take a trip to the mail room to see what's just come in?" he proposed companionably, a spry old elf of a man whose sharp black eyes never lost their merry twinkle. "Who knows? Maybe you've got some more letters waiting from folks who want to be in that fashion clinic of yours. Maybe even one from a real, live man this time!"

"Oh, Billy Ray, I hope so!" Lorna exclaimed earnestly as she rose to join him. Although it had not been difficult to find willing female subjects for her newly established "Before and After Fashion Clinic," securing men, especially in Larksborough, was a different matter entirely. Fashion was the furthest thing from the minds of most local men; although Lorna, in her latest article, had encouragingly suggested that they step forward and contact her, she had not yet received a single male response. Not that she was surprised. Subjects for the fashion clinic were supposed to be taken by Lorna herself on an extensive shopping tour where they were outfitted in clothing to complement and enhance their particular coloring, figure type and way of life. They were to receive grooming tips and advice on hair styling from Lorna, too, and the results of all of this would be documented by the *Courier* with a full page of coverage, including photographs. No, it did not surprise Lorna that the lo-

cal men were avoiding the fashion clinic, but surely there must be at least one man out there who
was progressive enough to volunteer. She certainly hoped so, especially since Roger was showing peevish signs of dissatisfaction. Readership
would broaden, he felt, if the fashion clinic
covered both sexes instead of only one.

So, Lorna's walk to the mail room with Billy
Ray was a somewhat anxious one, although the
little man beside her kept up a droll and diverting
series of remarks along the way.

"How about a stick of gum?" he suggested with
a wink, offering her one from his pocket. "I'm
getting hooked on it, I can tell you. It's one thing I
can chew around here without getting the evil eye
from you know who."

Lorna smiled at what had become a private
joke between them. When she had accidentally
discovered Billy Ray chewing tobacco in his little
cubbyhole of an office, the initial ice between
them had thawed completely. "Caught red-
handed!" Billy Ray had muttered grumpily. "I
hope you don't run and tell Roger on me; he
doesn't set store by tobacco chewing, and I guess
you don't, either, being as it doesn't look very
up-and-coming." Lorna, though, suddenly
touched by the plight of this funny little man, had
taken his side. "I won't say a word, Mr. Turner,"
she promised him in a lighthearted whisper. "Besides, my father chews tobacco, so you make me
feel right at home!" Ever since then, she and Billy
Ray had been both fellow conspirators and
friends at work.

They arrived in the mail room where the diminutive Billy Ray stood on tiptoe to reach for the correspondence in Lorna's mailbox. Not that she, with her willowy height, couldn't have done it with far less trouble. Billy Ray, though, enjoyed such little displays of gallantry.

"Looky here!" he exclaimed after a few moments of interested examination. "Here's a letter from the big man himself—Grady McGraw at Southern Tech!" He let out a whistle as he placed it in Lorna's hand. "Go ahead and open it, why don't you? Could be just what you've been waiting for!"

Lorna stared at it in surprise. Perhaps Billy Ray was right; why else would she be receiving this letter, its return address plainly indicating that it had come from the athletic department at Southern Tech? And Grady McGraw, whose name was printed on the envelope, was an important person there. The basketball coach, she seemed to recall, or was it football? She no longer remembered, but it didn't seem important. What mattered was the contents of the letter. She removed it from the envelope and began to read it avidly.

"Dear Miss Lambert," it said. "I hope you will let me be in your fashion clinic. As you say in your articles, a positive image is important, and I need your help in improving mine. As the head football coach of the Rebels, I am often asked to speak before groups, and I also appear once a week on the locally broadcast TV show 'North Carolina Replay.' That is why I would like your help. Please contact me as soon as possible, since I am

eagerly looking forward to working with you."
Beneath this, scrawled in black ink, was the name
Grady McGraw.

Lorna couldn't have been more delighted. The
letter was a small miracle, one that had arrived in
her hands at just the right moment! Billy Ray,
though, after reading the letter himself, seemed
to be somewhat mystified. "From what I know of
McGraw, I'd say he was the last man on earth to
give two hoots about fashion." He chuckled
knowingly. "Are you sure you didn't soften him
up by batting your eyelashes at him just a little
bit?"

"Billy Ray, I don't even know the man"—
Lorna laughed in protest—"so you can't accuse
me of any such tricks. Besides, why shouldn't he
be interested in improving his image? He's in the
public eye a lot, so it's perfectly natural that he's
turning to the fashion clinic for advice. That's
what it's for, and I'm just glad to think he realizes
it."

"Well, if you knew him like I did, you might be
surprised yourself," Billy Ray explained wryly.
"But come to think of it, he's been out of town for
the past few weeks, so I guess you haven't had the
chance to run into him yet. If you had, you'd
remember. There's only one Grady McGraw; no
mistake about it." He studied the letter again with
a baffled shake of his head. "I guess I don't know
him like I thought I did, but if you want an
introduction, I'd be happy to oblige. Why don't
you come with me to the college field house this
afternoon? I've got to speak to some of the folks

in the athletic department, so I'll be glad to introduce you to McGraw. He's a real friendly fellow, but he's got a long way to go before being a fashion plate." Billy Ray looked up at Lorna with a smile. "That doesn't mean you can't show him the light. I reckon that's what this is all about!"

Shortly after lunch, Lorna found herself in territory that was completely unknown to her. A practice was underway inside the football stadium at Southern Tech. To her uncomprehending eyes, though, it looked like an exercise in wasted energy. As soon as the Rebels began to run through plays on the field, it seemed as though they were collapsing on one another in a tumbled heap on the ground. Wasn't the object of the game to hang on to the ball? Lorna wondered. If so, she had lost sight of it among this heap of bodies. Billy Ray, however, was watching everything with a full measure of appreciation.

"Good play!" he exclaimed, his eyes never leaving the field. "McGraw's really whipping those boys into shape; they're sure to score points like that all season long."

Lorna listened in silence. This was a rough-and-tumble world that she knew nothing about, mostly because she had always stayed far away from it. Football just didn't appeal to her, and the fascination it held for others eluded her completely. Now she watched the players rise from their heap in response to the shrill call of a whistle. They were armored so heavily with bulky padding underneath their green and yellow uniforms that they appeared brutish to Lorna's eyes. Even their faces, hidden behind the metal bars of their helmets, hardly seemed human. She frowned, shading her eyes from the sun as she tried to find the one person in the crowd whom she had come there to see. For the moment, though, she couldn't seem to discern one from another.

Billy Ray did not have the same problem. "There's your man McGraw," he told her as he pointed to a tall, strapping figure who was approaching the team in the manner of a commanding general about to address his troops. "You can't miss him. With that red hair of his, he stands right out from the crowd."

For a moment, Lorna stared ahead in unblinking silence, but soon enough she was filled with such a rush of delighted surprise that she heard herself laughing aloud. "But he's—he's the man called Night Train!" she blurted out in amazement.

"That's right." Billy Ray nodded. "He's Grady 'Night Train' McGraw to be exact, a title he earned for himself during his days in pro football. Best linebacker the Dallas Cyclones ever had. So good that his opponents likened him to a night train that came rushing at them from out of nowhere." Billy Ray chuckled as he popped a stick of gum into his mouth. "But I thought you said you didn't know him."

"I do, though! I met him at the paper a few weeks ago, but he—well, he just never told me who he was." Lorna felt herself flush with embarrassment. She hadn't really wanted to know who he was, of course, and now she felt more than a little foolish for dismissing him so blindly. That he was the football coach at Southern Tech explained everything, though. His football game with the men from the print shop had been just a friendly gesture on his part, while his meeting with Roger Haskell, instead of concerning a labor dispute, must have revolved around the column that he wrote for the *Courier*. Yes, she certainly should have known better, but in spite of her shortsightedness, no real harm had been done. Far from it, in fact. She and this man were still friends, so much so that she had converted him to her way of thinking! Lorna smiled with shining eyes. She had found a male subject for the fashion clinic at that, a man of such local prominence that an article about him would be quite a feather in her cap!

"Well, since you've already met each other, I guess I don't have to stick around for introductions," Billy Ray was chortling good-naturedly. "Like I said, I've got some other folks to see, so I'll be on my way—if that's all right with you."

At Lorna's nod, he began to amble toward the field house with a pad of paper in his hand. As kind as his offer of help had been, she didn't need him now, Lorna told herself happily. She and Grady "Night Train" McGraw were friends, and their friendship had evidently taken a most promising turn.

"Take four laps around the field, men," she heard him order his players in a sharp, brisk tone of authority that she had never heard him use before. "And snap to it! If I see anyone dragging their feet, they'll get four more laps before they can head for the showers. All right, move now and move fast!"

Several of the Rebels groaned audibly, but they obeyed him just the same. Soon enough, the entire squad had formed a moving procession of green and mustard as the players jogged around the field. At first, their coach eyed them keenly, but the lines of his tall body relaxed after a few minutes, when it became clear that the practice was drawing to a satisfactory close. Surely, Lorna thought, it was the perfect time to let him know that she was here. She began stepping toward him in a mood of bubbling anticipation.

Of course, she did feel a little out of place on the football field in her high-heeled sandals and a jacketed dress of pale blue linen. But how was she to have known that morning that she would be running such a delightful errand later in the day? She approached McGraw with a smile on her face before he turned to look her way.

"Well, hi!" he greeted her warmly, taking in the sight of her with a look of marked appreciation. "This is a pleasant surprise, Miss Lambert. I must say that I never figured you for a football fan."

Then she was laughing, just as she always seemed to be doing when she was with him. Oh, how good to see him again! His face broke into one of his most endearing grins, and she was aware of the bracing vitality that emanated from his presence. "Hello," she replied. "You're right, you know. I'm no football fan, but I guess you must know why I'm here."

A reddish-gold eyebrow lifted in surprise, while he continued to regard her without saying a word. He was teasing her, no doubt, simply waiting for her to tell him that she had received his letter so that he could enjoy her response. And in her excitement she most certainly did not plan on letting him down!

"I'm so happy to think that you're going to be in my new fashion clinic, Coach McGraw," she began in a rush. Then she stopped herself breathlessly. "Maybe I should call you Mr. McGraw or—or even Grady, if that's all right with you."

Still, he gave no answer, and his suddenly guarded expression was beginning to make her feel uneasy. Why didn't he say something, anything, or did he want her to deliver a nonstop monologue instead? Well, perhaps he did, if only to hear the lively plans that had been formulating in her mind all morning long.

"I'm sure you'll be pleased with your new image, and our readers will be, too," she went on with brave determination. "Of course, you are an unusually big man, but that's no reason why we can't outfit you in well-fitting clothing. Hewitt's on Main Street carries a fine line of extra-large sizes for men, everything from imported suits to hand-woven sweaters and some especially nice leather topcoats." She paused, thinking that he would be pleased to hear this. She saw no pleasure in his narrowed eyes, though, while his usually smiling mouth seemed frozen in grimness.

Nevertheless, Lorna went on, too nervous to stop herself and feeling, too, that an enthusiastic response from him was surely only moments away. "We'll also want to make an appointment with a good hair stylist," she continued with a hopeful smile. "Your hair could certainly use a trim in any case, and it's so thick that it will help to have it layered. With a good cut, you'll find it very manageable and easy to care for, and since you're so busy, I'm sure you'll appreciate that very much." She was babbling now, but she couldn't seem to stop. If only he would say something to break his stony silence! But he said nothing, causing Lorna to feel herself gripped by a cold and sinking sense of doom. "I'm sure you'll find that a good haircut will do wonders for you," she concluded desperately.

She saw that his arms were folded implacably against his chest, while his eyes were snapping with rage. "You've got your nerve," he told her slowly, his anger surfacing like the first rumbles of a volcanic eruption. "You may not like me the way I am, but that gives you no right to march in here and order me to change. I told you the last time we met that I didn't go in for a lot of fancy packaging; only you didn't want to leave it at that, did you? Now I know why the people at the paper call you 'Princess.' It's a name you've earned for yourself in every way."

His words lashed her like a whip, and for a moment, Lorna had the sense that she was reeling, her shaky legs tottering as if they would no longer keep her in balance. What was he saying, and even more awful, why was he saying it? "But—but you told me that you wanted this, that you wanted to be in the fashion clinic." Her voice sounded faint, bewildered.

"I said no such thing, and you know it. I'm not about to become putty in anyone's hands, least of all yours, with your holier-than-thou airs. Now look, this is my turf. I suggest you get out of here before I throw you out."

Lorna's shock was beginning to give way to a fury of her own. He did, indeed, mean everything he said, having lured her there for no other reason, evidently, than to ridicule her without mercy. Well, she would not play the role of victim any longer. She would gladly punch him in the nose, but she heard herself hurling a string of angry charges at him instead. "You've got to be the most loathsome, underhanded, despicable man I've ever met. And if this is your idea of a joke"—she reached inside her purse for the letter and slapped it in his hand—"then you should be hung from the rafters! Don't worry about my leaving. I don't intend to stand here and take this one minute longer."

Nor did she. She spun around abruptly and walked off the field with her head held high and her heart beating like a wild bird within her breast. At least she was leaving him far behind, the growing distance between them her only salvation. Finally, she reached her car in the parking lot and sank into it as though she were taking sanctuary. The other cars around her and the nearby stadium were blurs before her eyes, whirling around her like disconnected objects in a senseless nightmare.

She put her hands over her eyes to shut everything out of view. Did the other people at the paper really call her "Princess" behind her back? Why? They hardly knew her and hadn't even given her a fair chance. Far worse than even that, however, was the turncoat behavior of Coach Grady McGraw, her Mr. Night Train, whom she had believed to be a friend. Oh, how wrong she was, and how completely he had betrayed her! It hurt, too, so painfully that she could not keep the tears from spilling down her cheeks. She shouldn't, of course, shed a single tear over a man so ruthless and uncaring, but she couldn't seem to help it. How could anyone who once seemed so full of goodness reveal such cruelty beneath his surface?

Lorna was only barely aware that a figure was approaching her. Soon enough, though, she realized with a sinking heart that it was Grady McGraw himself, come to see her for God only knew what hateful purpose. She turned her face away as she heard him open the door and enter her car, where he seated himself without a word.

"I'm sorry," he said at last. "I'm so awfully sorry."

"Please leave," she managed to reply in a choked voice, keeping her head turned from him so that he would not know she had been crying. "It's too late for an apology. There's—there's nothing left to say."

"Yes, there is." His voice was urgent, and the gentle touch of his hand on her shoulder felt like kindness itself. "You see, I didn't write that damned letter. I don't know who did—some practical joker at the paper, maybe—but when I get my hands on him, I'll—"

At this, Lorna turned around in surprise to meet a pair of blue-green eyes that suddenly filled with compassion. "Oh, God, you've been crying," he moaned softly. "Please don't cry. I can't stand to see you do that." Then he was fumbling in one of his pockets, from which he retrieved a clean but crumpled handkerchief. "Here, we'll wipe away those tears, and then we'll try to forget them. He began to sponge them painstakingly from her face with small, flurried movements that seemed out of keeping with his sheer size and strength. "Please don't worry yourself about it anymore. The joke was on both of us, and we'll just have to sort of rise above it. Are you going to be okay now, Lorna?" He stopped himself at the softly uttered mention of her name. "Maybe we can be on a first-name basis now. It'll be one way of putting that joker in his place; besides, I never liked that 'Miss Lambert' stuff, anyway. Unless you do, of course," he added hastily. "I mean, I'll call you whatever name you like."

Lorna giggled. She had been right about him, after all, and in his concern for her, he was funny and touching. Such a big, strapping man he was, but so surprisingly tender, too! There was not enough room for his long legs in her small car, she saw, so he had been forced to position them awkwardly, reminding her of a gentle visiting giant who was too kind to complain to his hostess about his cramped accommodations. She laughed softly. "Please call me Lorna. I'd like that very much."

"And I'm Grady." One of his lopsided grins was spreading warmly across his face in response to her laughter. Then his eyes fell to the handkerchief that he still held in his hand. "I know this isn't the fanciest thing," he said, chuckling, "but if you get me into the fashion clinic, then I'm sure to wind up with a different one for each day of the week, all of them bearing my initials and a designer label to boot."

"Let's just forget the fashion clinic, Grady." Lorna sighed wearily. "I know that you're not interested and—"

"Well, maybe I could help you out, anyway. Unless you've got a long list of men who just can't wait for their turn to come."

Lorna did not reply. She had no men for the fashion clinic, of course, and to make matters worse, Roger had been pressuring her to find one soon. The man beside her, though, his hand still warm on her shoulder, seemed to sense her dilemma.

"Look, Lorna, you'll never be able to turn me into a prize-winning beauty, but I want you to know that I am a good sport. Since you need help, I'll volunteer. Dress me up any way you want to, and I promise not to say a word. I'll even smile as pretty as you please for the camera."

He would at that, Lorna concluded from the generous concern that she read in his smiling eyes. Except that his heart would not be in it. "You really don't have to do me any favors," she protested. "This isn't your fault and—"

"Let me, Lorna," he coaxed her, his deep, gruff voice falling to a beguiling whisper. "Never be too proud to accept a favor from a friend. And I am your friend. At least I'd like to be. You believe me, don't you?"

Suddenly, all of the pain and disappointment of her day vanished. She was aware only that the big, rough-hewn man beside her was offering her a gift that seemed to come straight from his heart. "I do believe you," she murmured softly. "And I—I will accept an offer from a friend."

Something touched his face—a ray of light, perhaps—that softened its hard planes with an amber glow. She was aware too, of a muscle that twitched in his cheek and that he was drawing closer, the bracing aura of his body filling her senses. Then, like a pledge that was all the sweeter for having been so unexpected, he was kissing her, his lips nuzzling hers slowly and with such a warm current of feeling that it began to rush through her veins. Oh, how good this felt, like the promise of new life to come! For a time, it was only their softly moving mouths that joined them, but soon his arms were enfolding her, pulling her tightly against his muscular chest, while her hands found him, too, seeking to bring him even nearer. When she felt the tip of his tongue part her lips, she could not stop him. She could only welcome him instead as something throbbed and quickened within her. For this moment, at least, his embrace was a haven of beguiling warmth, and she had the odd, sweet feeling that she had come home at last.

Finally, he pulled away, while her eyes, full of a hundred unanswered questions, searched his softly. "Isn't this a strange beginning for a friendship, Grady?"

"It's the best way to begin," he assured her with a slow smile. "With a start like this, there's no telling how far our friendship will take us."

And that, of course, was just the problem, Lorna worried, as she considered it later. It had happened so fast that she scarcely knew what had hit her. All she knew was that she had collided with a man called Night Train, not as a friend but as a lover, and that there seemed to be no earthly reason for it. The two of them had nothing in common; soon, in fact, she would be confronted by the challenge of having to create some sort of new and fashionable image for him, an undertaking that he would endure as though it were a vastly amusing joke. In fact, Grady McGraw, for all of his diamond-in-the-rough charm, was not the right sort of man for her. He knew and cared nothing about the kind of work she did, while she couldn't even begin to understand his. They were simply opposites in every way, and once they spent more than half an hour in each other's company, they were sure to reach a dead end when it came to shared values and mutual points of view. Why, then, had his kiss fed such a longing within her, and why had it left her with the absurdly blissful sense that for now, all was right in the world?

Chapter Four

The shorn strands of his copper-colored hair lay scattered about him on the floor as Grady observed the results of his newly styled haircut in a hand mirror. An elusive cat-that-swallowed-the-canary grin flickered about the corners of his generous mouth.

Lorna waited for him to show some further response, as did the young woman called Christine, the chief stylist at Larksborough's most fashionable salon who had worked so painstakingly to create this flattering new haircut for him. Nevertheless, Grady remained maddeningly silent, not with any real sense of disapproval, Lorna could tell, but as if he were privately savoring a good joke that he was not about to share with anyone.

"That is what you had in mind, isn't it, sir?"

asked Christine with an anxious frown, the blow drier still in her hands.

He shrugged pleasantly, his teasing eyes falling upon Lorna. "Well, you'll have to ask the boss here. She's the one who knows best."

The "boss," though, sighed under her breath, barely concealing the twinges of annoyance that he was beginning to make her feel. It was, after all, his haircut that was in question, not hers. He was the one who would be wearing it, and while she hardly expected him to shout for joy, he could show at least a little bit of interest in his new appearance. It certainly was an improvement, and under Christine's skillful hands, his unruly shock of hair had been tamed, falling into place now in smooth, glossy waves that made an elegant frame for the craggy features of his face.

"I like it very much," Lorna told Christine with an appreciative nod. "And I especially like what you've done up here. It was so tangled before that I was afraid it might never lie flat."

Christine smiled, glad that her best efforts had not gone unnoticed. "His hair does seem to have a will of its own, doesn't it? But a little layering always helps, along with that new conditioner I used. In fact, he ought to take a bottle home with him. I'd like to see him apply it after each shampoo."

Although he was being discussed as if he weren't in the room, Grady did not seem to mind. Nor did he make any effort to include himself in the conversation. He simply sat resignedly in his chair, the lines of his long body relaxed and passive, his booted feet planted firmly on the floor. Lorna sighed again. He was enduring this whole venture as she had feared he would, good-naturedly enough but waiting only for the tedium to come to an end. It wouldn't have to be so dull for him, Lorna thought irritably, if he would just show some personal interest in what was taking place for his own benefit. Of course, it was for Lorna's benefit, too, as the *Courier's* new fashion writer, that he had agreed to come in the first place. That didn't mean though, that he couldn't derive something positive from the experience.

"I hope you will consider using the conditioner on a regular basis," Lorna told him, hoping to coax a few glimmers of enthusiasm from him. Just look at what it's done for you already! That cowlick of yours is lying down, and it doesn't look as though it's going to give you any more trouble."

His palm went to the top of his head in a futile search for something that was no longer there. "Oh, but I think I'm going to miss it," he said in a tone of playful melancholy. "I always thought of it as my most distinguishing feature. Besides, how will I be able to recognize myself without it?"

His eyes twinkled sharply, and for a moment he seemed nearly ready to share his secret joke with her. Lorna, though, saw no reason to encourage him. It was all very well and good to laugh, of course, but not at the expense of having this trip, which she had planned so carefully, degenerate into a farce. "Well, you shouldn't have any trouble recognizing yourself," she said briskly. "New haircut or not, I'd say you're still pretty much one of a kind." Somehow, those words came out sounding almost like a reprimand, and for a second their eyes met in a spirit of tense and underlying challenge. Then Lorna looked away quickly, her eyes falling to her wristwatch. "Anyway, we should be leaving now. We've still got lots of shopping to do at Hewitt's, and I've arranged to have the photographer meet us there in just a little while."

Grady drew in a long breath before he let it out in an equally long sigh. Still, he did not openly protest, and soon enough his face masked over with that curiously bland and blameless expression. No, Lorna really could not accuse him of being a bad sport. He was abiding fairly and squarely by all the rules she had set; that he was merely going through the motions of the game could not be held against him. It was, of course, not his game. Nevertheless, Lorna could not help but wish that it was. How much simpler things would be that way!

Having been released from his chair, Grady soon stood lounging in the doorway of the salon where he patiently waited for Lorna to join him. She found herself detained briefly by Christine, who handed her the bottle of hair conditioner with a knowing wink and a few confidentially spoken words of advice. "He's the type of guy who can be a pretty tough customer, isn't he? But I wouldn't worry too much about changing him if I were you. I think he's pretty darn cute just like he is!"

And exasperating, too, Lorna added silently as she turned to meet him, thinking how much he resembled a restless schoolboy with nothing but

secret mischief up his sleeve. Did he take anything seriously, or did he merely laugh at life as
though it were an endless comedy? He probably
did, and the thought was disconcerting. It could
only mean that he regarded all the things that
were so important to her as further sources of
entertainment. Oh, yes, he had a certain offbeat
appeal, but for some reason, that fact only irritated Lorna more. If it weren't for his disarming,
unconventional charm, she probably never would
have allowed herself to be drawn into this crazy
situation in the first place.

But it was too late for regrets. Roger Haskell
had already scheduled her article on the transfor-
mation of Grady McGraw for the Wednesday
edition of the paper, while the manager at
Hewitt's, eager for the publicity, was expecting
them shortly. No, there was no turning back, and
as Lorna thought of what lay ahead, she was sure
that she had her work cut out for her. During her
consultation with Grady earlier in the day, she
had been able to determine little except that he
wore his sweatshirts and rumpled khakis as a
virtual uniform about town. He dressed in those
outfits for all occasions, even his weekly TV show
and his other public appearances, too. "I've gotten used to them, and they've gotten used to me,"
he had explained with one of his lopsided grins.
"Old clothes are like old friends, sort of comfortable and easy to be with. At least that's my
opinion, but I suppose you have one of your
own."

She did, indeed; so different from his that she
was nearly at a loss to try and explain it to him.

Sweatshirts and khakis were fine, of course, on a few occasions. But they were not appropriate when a good impression was necessary and when a person was in the public spotlight. Apparently, Grady McGraw, in spite of his former career in the glamorous world of professional football, had a long way to go before understanding this basic rule.

A low-keyed, gradual approach would probably work best, she cautioned herself. True, she would have to outfit him in a properly tailored suit, but before that took place, she would ease him into a receptive state of mind. The next stop, therefore, was to the section at Hewitt's where casual men's wear was on display. There, in an atmosphere of subdued background music, tastefully paneled walls and sales clerks who spoke in hush and courteous tones of voice, Grady would be free to find apparel that would not depart too drastically from what he usually wore.

He seemed, though, to be as disinterested and as faintly amused as before, following her brisk movements with a prankish smile and whistling offhandedly as well. Nor did he pay any real attention to the displays of attractive clothing. With barely a glance, he took in the sight of the sweaters that were piled high on a table before he fixed his eyes on Lorna.

"You're not going to make me try on any of these things, are you? I mean, my sweatshirts keep me warm enough."

"Well, the point is that you can be warm and style conscious at the same time," Lorna began carefully. "One of these sweaters with a pair of those trousers on the rack would give you a nice, casual outfit to wear around town, don't you think?"

He sighed. "You don't leave any stone unturned, do you, boss? Well, you can go ahead and make the selections. Between the two of us, I'd say you're the one with the fancier taste."

Lorna counseled herself to be patient. At least she had gotten him this far in body, if not in spirit, and it would be foolish to expect much more from him for now. Besides, his willingness to let her make all of the choices would give her free reign in matters of style and color. That would be a welcome challenge, and she brightened at the promising possibilities that seemed to lie in store.

"Well, I think this would be flattering on you," she began as she selected a sweater from the stack. Of moss green wool, the pullover was handsomely knit, distinguished by a bold cable design and crew-neck styling. But as she held it up against his chest to see if it would fit him, she momentarily forgot the business at hand. There was something frankly intimate about choosing clothes for a man, especially when the man was Grady McGraw. Next to him, she felt almost diminutive, although at five feet seven she was far from that. Grady, though, was much taller than she and so broadly build and well muscled that Lorna, with her fine-boned slenderness, felt fragile by comparison. She stepped back somewhat, even as she was aware of his scent, that woodsy blend of pine and sunshine that he always seemed to bring with him from the out-of-doors.

"This sweater should fit you quite nicely," she told him, trying to get down to business. "And it compliments your eyes and hair, too. Green is definitely your color, you know."

"Do you think so?" He chuckled nonchalantly, holding the sweater against him as he ambled to a three-way mirror. "Well, you could be right, boss. All I need is a hat with a feather before I start to look like an overgrown leprechaun." Then, seeing that Lorna was not amused, he laughingly tried to make amends. "A respectable one, of course. A real pillar of the leprechaun community."

In spite of herself, Lorna could not keep from laughing, too. Maybe he was a kind of leprechaun at that. It seemed as likely an explanation for his disarming behavior as any other that she could think of. Nevertheless, it filled her with a sense of frustration. How could she, her knowledge of fashion notwithstanding, be expected to bring about any significant change in this man's appearance? A whole new wardrobe of costly, distinguished clothing would do nothing to dim the bright lights of irreverence that twinkled in his eyes. And his hair, whether styled or not, was of such a unique and arresting shade of red that it was bound to mark him forever as a maverick, a man meant to go through life in his own way and on his own unorthodox terms.

Well, she still had her job to do, and she would simply have to do the best she could. Soon she was bustling about the department, aided by the sales clerks, who obligingly held her selections for her and who agreed, when Grady finally tried them on, that they looked very well on the gentleman, indeed. The gentleman, however, remained disinterested in their comments, and although he did not actively resist playing the role of fashion model, it was clear that he took no great joy from it, either.

"How about a little time off for good behavior, boss? We must have been here all day long."

Lorna sighed. Actually, they had been there for just an hour. During that time Grady had behaved with the same sense of obligation that he might have reserved for a dental appointment. His true colors emerged only in the company of the *Courier*'s photographer, Wayne Dykes, a man who seemed as amused as he did by what was taking place and with whom he joked outrageously. Such comments as "Tell me I'm gorgeous, Wayne" and "If I don't win the next game by being tough, then I'm sure to win it by being beautiful!" had enlivened all of his poses before the photographer. No, he still refused to take any of this seriously in spite of Lorna's best efforts, and she was beginning to get a headache.

"Look, Grady," she told him with exasperation, keeping her voice low enough so that the nearby sales clerks would not overhear, "just don't make things any more difficult than they already are. We still have to select a suit for you, and—"

He groaned. "No, we don't. I never wear suits if I can help it, so I'd say it's about time to call it a day."

"Not quite yet," she said, firmly folding her arms across her chest. "It seems to me that you have ample opportunities in your life to wear a suit, and I won't let you leave here without one." Aware that his patience was beginning to wear thin, she tried to soften her words. "It shouldn't take very long. I promise you that we'll be finished in just a little while.

Fortunately, she turned out to be right. Choosing a suit for Grady was not difficult, and it was simplified by the fact that he took no part whatsoever in the selection. The sales clerk's solicitous question of whether the gentleman would prefer something in brown, gray or blue did not even have to be considered. Grady simply didn't care, enabling Lorna to make the choice by herself. He had looked fine in the brightly colored sports clothes that she had selected, but now she deliberately aimed for a conservative contrast. Soon enough she had found it in a three-piece pin-striped suit of navy blue wool, which bore a designer label and all of the artful details of European styling. With its air of quiet elegance, it was the kind of suit that she especially admired, the kind that Roger Haskell often wore, in fact. She only hoped that Grady would try it on without a fuss.

Thankfully, he did, if only to bring his long ordeal to an end. When he disappeared into the dressing room, Lorna sighed with relief. She had managed, after all, to get through a most difficult assignment, and she was grateful that it had not been worse than it was.

Her head still ached, though, and she was barely prepared for the sight of Grady when he emerged from his dressing room in the navy blue suit. She had expected him to look good in it, of course—she had chosen it for that purpose—but she saw with a rush of admiration and delighted surprise that he looked far better than good. He looked, in fact, nothing short of magnificent. Navy blue was his color even more so than green, for it both enhanced and subdued the vivid color of his hair and eyes. All signs of his rough edges had disappeared, while the elegant lines of the suit emphasized the width of his shoulders, his tapered waist and the splendid length of his strong, lean legs. He might have been a business tycoon of international renown in this master-piece of fine tailoring; certainly, it set him head and shoulders above all other men whom Lorna had ever seen. She was far too pleased to keep her excitement from him.

"Grady, just look at you!" she exclaimed with a broad smile. "And don't say another word about how you don't like to wear suits. You just can't afford not to wear them, not when they make you look like this!"

"I was afraid you might like it," he said testily. "I suppose it fits all your notions of the way you think I should look."

"Well, yes, it does, but what's wrong with that? It makes you look distinguished and important and—well, I think you've found your image, after all. That was the whole point of this trip, remember?"

"Not as I remember it," he said. "I agreed to come along, but a new image was the furthest thing from my mind. To tell you the truth, my intentions are the same as when we first started." Then, much to her embarrassment, he tweaked her nose, while the sales clerk looked on curiously, a polite smile masking his confusion.

Lorna stepped away. Why did he have to bring that up now? If any proof was needed that Grady McGraw could look distinguished and sophisticated, then the suit provided it beyond all shadow of doubt. Why couldn't he seem to care, if only just a little, and why must he dismiss it as such a foolish joke?

But at least he voiced no real objections to adding the suit to his wardrobe. Soon enough, the tailor was pinning it at the cuffs for the necessary alterations before Wayne Dykes stepped forward with a wry smile to complete his final set of photographs.

When the last flashbulb had popped, Grady turned to Lorna with a lazy grin. "Well, boss, I played by your rules, just like I said. Are you ready to play by mine?"

She watched him warily. "And just what is that supposed to mean?"

"Let me get changed first," he told her with a wink, "and then you'll find out all about it."

He disappeared into the dressing room, his spirits buoyed by whatever secret plan he had in mind. When he appeared a few minutes later, though, he looked the same as he had when Lorna had first seen him in the *Courier*'s parking lot. It was as though he had never gone shopping with her at all. Rather than wearing one of the stylishly casual new outfits that Lorna had selected for him, he had reverted, predictably, to his loose-fitting brown sweatshirt and his rumpled pair of khaki pants. Oh, the absolute futility of this whole day! And what was he trying to tell her by appearing in his scruffy old clothes? Only that he frankly thought her advice ridiculous and that he intended to disregard it completely.

Even so, he showed no signs of resentment. In fact, his manner was more disarming than ever. "Come on now, Lorna," he coaxed her. "You're not going to hold this against me, are you? It isn't that I don't appreciate your good taste and all, but you have to understand that I like to give my new clothes a chance to mellow before I wear them. It's a matter of breaking them in, you might say."

Lorna frowned, suspecting that he was merely pulling the wool over her eyes. "I never heard of anything like that, Grady. Besides, what good will those clothes do you by hanging in your closet? I don't think you're going to wear them at all."

"And what if I don't? I thought we reached an agreement the other day—live and let live. You haven't forgotten it, have you?" He placed his arm lightly about her slender shoulders and looked into her blue eyes with a smile that suddenly caused her anger to dissolve into a pool of softness. It made no sense that she should respond to him in such a way, but nothing about her relationship with him made any sense, including the kiss they had shared the other day. She recalled it in a vivid rush, and as she gazed back at him, she knew that he was remembering it, too.

"We're going to have ourselves some real fun, Lorna," he murmured softly. "I'd like to take you to a place where you'll meet the finest people in town."

That sounded like a promising-enough invitation, and Lorna didn't want to turn him down. Still, she felt confused. If he wished to take her to Beauchamp's Restaurant or perhaps even to the country club, where dinner and dancing were featured every Friday night, then he was not dressed properly. "I'd like to go, Grady, but don't you think you'd better put on something different, for heaven's sake?" Then she laughed at the thought of how she must look herself. It had been a long day, and although her outfit—a smart pair of tapered trousers topped by a brown silk blouse and a caramel-colored jacket—still looked presentable enough, she was sure that the rest of her did not. She found, in fact, with a flurried pat on her head, that strands of her hair had strayed untidily from her chignon, while her makeup, applied so carefully in the morning, was undoubtedly in need of repair. "Anyway, I'd really like to freshen up before we go," she told him.

He responded to her request with laughter, so contagious and filled with such a warm sense of joy that Lorna could not keep from laughing, too. "Neither of us will have to do that. Trust me on this one, Lorna. These people will like us just the way we are." Then he squeezed her hand and held it while he began leading her down an aisle in the department store that led outdoors. They laughed again for no particular reason, and even though Lorna still had no idea of where he was going to take her, it did not seem to matter. Wherever their destination, she had the glowing sense that she was about to have a perfectly wonderful time.

Chapter Five

Although Grady's jeep was sturdy, it provided no cushion whatsoever from each and every pothole that lay along the dusty trail. Beauchamp's Restaurant, as well as the country club, were both far behind; in fact, the jeep was now headed toward that part of town that offered few, if any, notable spots in which to spend an evening and where most of the roads were bumpy and uneven. Still, it seemed like a fitting-enough journey, Lorna told herself, considering the company she was in. Grady McGraw was a man who evidently steered clear of the plush conveniences that life had to offer; with him, she felt, the road would always be a rugged one.

Nevertheless, the familiar countryside was not really unpleasant. It was here that the buildings of

the town began to thin out, giving way to tall
green pines that grew densely along the road.
And because the autumn season was advanced,
the leafier trees that grew high on the hills were
changing color, splashed brightly with patches of
red and gold that might have been painted on
with an artist's brush.

Grady rounded another corner, passing the
shabby little grocery store known as Buster's,
which also doubled as a local post office. It was a
familiar sight to Lorna, for she had visited it many
times before, usually barefoot and in search of
penny candy during the long, hot summers of her
childhood. In fact, she knew every unremarkable
inch of the area by heart. Although Grady had
hinted of a destination that was "far off the
beaten track," there was nothing unusual or
intriguing there that Lorna could see. And so they
traveled on, even as an absurd idea began to take
shape in her mind. Of all the places to go, he
really couldn't be planning to take her to that one,
could he?

Her question was answered for her in a matter
of minutes. Yes, he could. In fact, he was. Gravel
crunched beneath the tires of his jeep as they
pulled into a parking lot that was all too familiar
to her. Lorna stared ahead, too surprised for the
moment to say a word. She had come a long way
for herself in the world, but there she was, back
where she had started, at the ramshackle site of
Mack and Annie's Diner!

Then her surprise gave way to a disturbing
sense of suspicion. "Grady, are you trying to play
one of your crazy jokes on me?" she asked,

turning to him defensively. If so, she certainly
wasn't about to be the brunt of it!

"It's no joke, Lorna," he explained. "It may
not look like much from the outside, but don't let
that bother you. Inside, you'll get the best home-
style southern cooking that there is for miles
around. Besides, I want to introduce you to Mack
and Annie—they're the last of their kind, the real
salt of the earth, as far as I'm concerned. When
all is said and done, this place is quite a find."

Lorna watched him carefully. No, he was not
kidding. Strangely enough, he seemed to be as
fully sincere as he was unaware of what the diner
meant to her. She drew a long breath, knowing
that she would have to enlighten him. To do so,
however, would not be easy. She looked away
from him, a blush rising to her cheeks as she
nervously twisted a button on her jacket. "You
won't have to introduce me to Mack and Annie,"
she heard herself say in a low, guarded tone of
voice. "You see, I already know them. I mean—
well, they're my parents."

He grinned incredulously, and the look in his
eyes was further proof that he did not believe a
word she said. "Come on, Lorna. Don't tell me
I'm joking, not when you're doing such a fine job
of it all by yourself."

"But I'm not joking. I—it's really true," she
persisted weakly. And ironic, too, she added to
herself, to have to prove it to him as though it
were a rare and distinct privilege. She was almost
tempted to leave well enough alone. It was, after
all, flattering to think that he could not believe
that she was Mack's and Annie's daughter. She

was, though. There was no escaping it, and under the circumstances, she would have to convince him that it was true.

"You see, my parents names are Mack and Annie Lambert, and I'm Lorna Lambert," she began slowly. From the back of her mind, she heard a taunting chorus of voices—"Mack and Annie's daughter—fetch me a glass of water!" Still, she went on, trying to drown those voices out with her own words. "My parents have been running the diner for as long as I can remember, even before I was born. So this is where I grew up. I used to wait tables here, and if you need any more proof—"

"No, I'll take your word for it," he interrupted as a delighted smile spread across his face. "Come to think of it, that's the best news I've had in a long time. I always figured there must be more to you than the touch-me-not lady that I saw on the surface. And now I know for sure. You come from good people, Lorna. That's something to be proud of."

"I know, Grady. That's very true, of course, but—" She stopped, certain that he did not truly understand. He had not grown up in Larksborough, and to him Mack and Annie were merely quaint examples of local color, their diner an offbeat spot that offered him amusement in his meanderings about town.

"But what, Lorna?" he persisted.

She looked ahead of her, at the cluttered signs in the window and at the sagging steps of the old front porch. "Well, look at this place, will you, Grady? It's been like this ever since I can remember. You'll have to admit that it isn't exactly the kind of 'home, sweet home' that anyone would be proud of."

He let this last remark go by, more intent, it seemed, on discovering the reasons that lay behind it. "So it doesn't bring back a lot of fond memories for you, is that it?"

She wondered bitterly why he even had to ask. "No, of course it doesn't. As a matter of fact, all I ever wanted was to get away from here." She paused, aware that he was waiting intently for her to continue, almost as if her response could unravel clues to a mystery that intrigued him. At least he was a good listener, and her next words tumbled out in a rush. "I guess that's why some things are so important to me. When I was a kid, I used to pour through fashion magazines, wishing that I was a fine lady like some of the people at the country club. Only I was just Lorna Lee Nobody in discount-store dresses and my sister Lucille's hand-me-downs. It wasn't a whole lot of fun, Grady, especially in a town like this."

There! A painful lump had risen in her throat, but it was too late to conceal it. She had just spilled out her life story without even intending to do so, revealing far more of her private self than she had yet dared to show to another human being.

Yet she could not be sorry, not when Grady's hand clasped hers so firmly. Even though he did not say a word, the sheer warmth of his touch told her that he understood and that he cared. That was all, but at this moment, it was more than enough.

"You're a woman now, Lorna," she heard him say after a long silence. His voice had taken on a hushed quality, while his face was grooved deeply with lines of solemn concern. As ever, though, there were lively lights of humor in his eyes, reassuring her that there was no problem in life that could not be overcome with laughter. "You know, I think it's time that you put your priorities in a different kind of order."

Somehow, those were not the words she had been expecting to hear. "What kind of order, Grady?" she asked with a puzzled frown. "I'm not sure I understand."

Then he began to trace his forefinger from the top of her high forehead to the slightly tilted tip of her nose. "Oh, Lorna," he murmured. Soon his hands had fallen to her shoulders, and he looked into her eyes with a mixture of desire and compassion that she had never seen before. "Maybe you don't understand now, but stay with me for a while. I'll show you what I mean."

His voice had grown husky, and she gazed back at him as though she had fallen under a spell. This was neither the time nor the place for him to take her in his arms again, but as he did, she could not pull away. There was such glad warmth in the haven of his arms, and a sense of comfort, too, that she seemed to crave so badly. For a moment, he just held her, his lips brushing softly against her hair and cheeks. Then something between them seemed to ignite, a dancing flame that had been kindled to sudden life by their nearness. His lips claimed hers, not gently this time but with a sense of heated urgency that was almost rough. It

seemed to spring from a deep well of feeling, as if
he had far more to give than could possibly be
contained. She felt it flow into her body, engulfing
her like a tide, while his strong arms pulled her
closer, as if he would never let her go. And when
his tongue began an intimate search into the
warm spaces of her mouth, she heard herself
moan with a rush of pleasure. Her lips parted
softly as she opened herself to him like a flower.

But she must not let this go on. It was broad
daylight, after all, and they were in the parking lot
of her parents' diner, of all unlikely places! Besides, it made no sense that Grady McGraw, after
having irritated her so badly at Hewitt's, could
now be causing her to respond with such crazy
abandon. She pulled away from him suddenly.

"Grady, we—we'd better go inside." She tried
unsuccessfully to smooth the loose ends of her
hair into place. "It's time for me to sample some
of that good, down-home cooking, remember?"

"Oh, that." His laughter was low and muffled.
"I almost forgot, but it's all your fault. You do
strange things to me, Lorna."

As he did to her, she thought with a little shiver
as they made their way inside the diner. He had
reached something deep within her that no one
had ever touched before, assaulting both her
senses and her heart. How odd, though, that he
could have such an effect on her when they looked
at things so differently. His hint that she somehow
had her priorities all mixed up was just one more
example of that fact. Suddenly, it began to exas-
perate her. She had done very well for herself by
placing her priorities in a certain order long

before. Certainly, she was not about to let him topple them abruptly like so many apples in a cart. If anyone needed to be straightened out about a few things, then it was Grady McGraw and most definitely not she.

It was a relief to enter the diner. Here, at least, life was as predictable as ever, the air filled with the comforting twangs of a familiar old country song. And Mack Lambert, who greeting them, made an ebullient host. Nothing, it seemed, was too good for his daughter and Coach Grady McGraw, and he nearly outdid himself to make them feel welcome. Not only did he clean off their table twice, but he refused to let them sit down until he had personally whisked off their chairs with a small broom. "You're my two favorite customers," he explained with a flourishing gesture when he presented them with icy glasses of water. "There may not be a red carpet to roll out around here, but you'll get special treatment just the same."

Lorna and Grady smiled at one another after he promptly took their order and darted off to the kitchen, no doubt with special instructions for Lorna's mother, the cook.

"I don't know another place in town where the service is this good," Grady remarked with a chuckle. "And for my money, the Friday night special can't be beat."

He meant every word he said, Lorna saw, while even stranger yet was that he actually regarded Mack and Annie's Diner as a desirable spot to take a woman on a date. Not that she minded being there, of course, but just the same, she was puzzled by Grady's taste. It was unusual, to say the least. She looked about her at the other customers, most of them millworkers who customarily frequented the place at that time of day. One of them, a great bear of a man known as Uncle Bob, stopped by their table to chat. "Howdy, Lorna Lee!" he boomed. He greeted Grady, too, and soon enough the two men were kidding one another and exchanging remarks about football. Lorna watched them both, although her eyes invariably settled on Grady. It was plain to see that he was a regular customer there, known and welcomed by one and all. There were other places in town where he could go, but for some reason, he had picked that one to become his favorite stomping ground.

Well, he appeared to be a man with a hearty appetite, and the food there was certainly plentiful. And good, too, for Annie Lambert, who prepared it all, was proud of having a skilled touch in the kitchen. In fact, the Friday night special delivered everything it promised and more. There was fried chicken, heaped high in a basket, each piece crisp, sweet and done to a turn. There were golden biscuits, too, cream gravy and Annie Lambert's own "Hopping John," a lively medley of black-eyed peas and rice, seasoned with the zest of red hot peppers. Moreover, the portions were unlimited. Grady ate two full helpings of everything, while Mack Lambert stood by, waiting eagerly to offer him more. It was no wonder, Lorna thought, that her parents made so little money. They were far too generous with their customers, and at these low prices, they virtually gave their meals away.

She was not surprised when her father admitted as much when he sat down briefly to join them.

"The truth of it is that the old stove out in the kitchen is pretty much of a goner," he said in his easygoing way. "Looks like we'll need a new one, but I don't have to tell you how much that will cost." Then he winked broadly at Lorna. "The time has come for another fund-raising barbecue and country-music jamboree, wouldn't you say?"

Lorna frowned. Whenever they were short of ready cash, which was often, her parents put on one of those gala shindigs in order to raise it. They had great fun in doing so, but all of the hard work involved was never worth the effort. Their prices were too low, and because they rarely attracted large-enough crowds, they were lucky if they managed to break even. She voiced her reservations as tactfully as she could, wishing that her parents would turn to more practical methods of raising money.

Grady, though, was openly enthusiastic. Not only did he think it a wonderful idea, but he volunteered to help, entering into the plans for the barbecue with obvious relish. "What you need, Mack, is some good publicity," he explained to Lorna's father. "I can mention it in my column for starters, and then I'll see to it personally that all of the players on my team stop by for a kind of autograph-signing session. And I'll be there, too, of course, to keep the boys in line." He laughed heartily. "In a football-crazy town like this, that should attract crowds from far and near."

Well, perhaps it would, Lorna thought hopefully. Anything was possible, and it was undeniably generous of Grady to take so much interest in Mack and Annie's Diner. Maybe all it needed was better promotion, although on that particular day, at least, news of the Friday night special evidently had gotten around. People were now waiting for tables, and soon Lorna and Grady rose, feeling that it was time for them to leave. Before they did, though, they stepped inside the steamy kitchen for a brief visit with Annie Lambert. Not that she had much time to chat during that busy hour, but Lorna didn't want to leave without telling her good-by. Her mother had to work so hard, and as far as her daughter could tell, she received few, if any, real rewards for her efforts.

"Thanks for a delicious dinner, mom," she said with an affectionate kiss. "Every bite of it was wonderful."

Annie Lambert laughed good-naturedly as she withdrew half a dozen sweet potato pies from her ancient oven. "Don't try to sweet talk me, Lorna Lee, because I'm too smart for that. You just picked at your food, child, without even trying that nice new bread pudding of mine." She wiped her hands on her apron, a short, middle-aged woman who was as plump as her daughter was willowy. "If you want to dash away without dessert, then I can't stop you, but your friend here happens to be a man with a fine appetite." She nodded with approval in Grady's direction.

"The poor thing still looks famished to me, and there's no reason to punish him just because you eat like a bird." Then, just as Lorna knew she would do, she placed one of her freshly baked pies in a box and handed it to her daughter. "You take this with you now and be sure to share it with your friend. It's still broad daylight outside, time enough for a little picnic in the fresh air. That's what I'd be doing myself if I were young and fancy free!"

"Mom, really, we're not hungry," Lorna protested. She knew, though, that it was hopeless. She rarely managed to leave the diner without more food than she could finish by herself, but in this case, at least, she would have someone to help her eat it.

"A big man like Grady McGraw needs looking after," her mother told her in confidential tones. "There aren't too many like him around, and if you want my advice, Lorna Lee—" She stopped herself with a knowing chuckle. "But I guess you don't, so I won't give it. Just have yourself a good time now, and come back this way before too long, you hear?"

Soon enough, Lorna was seated in Grady's jeep again, while he drove along a rutted country road with a faint smile creasing the corners of his mouth. The sweet potato pie gave off a tempting aroma, and as Lorna looked about her, she noticed the brilliance of the trees with their burnished autumn colors. Perhaps her mother had been right about a picnic. It was a glorious Indian summer day, and everything in sight was bathed in a mellow golden light from the sun.

There would not be many more days like this before winter finally came. Suddenly, it seemed to beckon her with its brightness, shining before her eyes like a rare and unexpected treasure.

There was a small stream nearby, and a picnic table, too. She was not disappointed when they arrived, nor was Grady. As ever, it was a scenic and peaceful spot. The gnarled old maple tree on the banks provided flickering shade from the sun, even as a few of its fiery leaves fell away slowly, fluttering without sound to the wild grass below.

"I don't know about you, Lorna, but I would have been happy to grow up in a place like this." Having finished his piece of pie, Grady now sat watching the rippling waters of the stream as a pensive quality softened the angular lines of his profile.

"Where did you grow up, Grady?" she asked him curiously.

"Oh, everywhere and nowhere . . ." For the first time, Lorna noticed a sharp edge of sadness in his laughter. "My family moved all over creation when I was a kid, always on the go from one place to another. I never liked it, but it was the way to the top of the corporate ladder for my father. When his company transferred him, he went, and he took the rest of us right along with him. Those were his terms, and I guess he did pretty well for himself. The only catch in the whole thing was that he died of hypertension at the age of forty-seven."

"I'm sorry," Lorna told him softly.

He was silent for a while, too caught up in his memories to speak. When he did at last, there was a note of deep conviction in his voice. "Well, I learned something from it. I refuse to live my life that way. There are more important things for me—finding people I care about, for one thing, and putting down roots." He turned to her slowly, his keen eyes narrowed against the rays of the sun, his lashes touched with gold. "I've been here for two years, and I like it. So much that I'd be willing to stay here for the rest of my life."

"Right here in Larksborough?" She wondered aloud. There was nothing wrong with it, of course, but the world offered so many more interesting, glamorous places. New York, Atlanta, Dallas—all fashionable cities that had always seemed so full of excitement to Lorna. Why would anyone willingly turn his back on places such as those to settle for life in Larksborough?

"That's right," he replied, a forceful undercurrent running through his words. "That's what I said, and that's what I meant."

Lorna did not answer. His words represented one more difference between them, and she didn't want to dwell upon that just now. It was too lovely an afternoon; besides, she found herself intrigued by the fact that Grady's reddish-gold hair blended into the autumn landscape. Everywhere else his vivid coloring stood out like a beacon. It was only here that he found his match, for his arresting appearance neither competed with the burnished colors of the Indian summer day nor overshadowed them. In fact, he seemed to be part of the season, and as she watched him, she felt sure that the bracing vitality of his presence had come from the same powerful source as the elements themselves. His blue eyes seemed to have been taken from the sky itself, while his skin was as golden as the sun. Even the rust-toned hair on his hands seemed one with the season. When she tried to tell him so, however, he was greatly amused.

"If color coordination is what makes you happy, then I'm in big trouble," he said with a broad grin. "I suppose when summertime comes around, you'll want me to dye my hair green."

She broke out into a ripple of laughter at his crazy words, her eyes sparkling with light and joy. Oh, it felt so good to laugh this way that she couldn't even care about how silly and childlike it must make her appear. For the time being, she was content to let the good feeling overtake her fully, carrying her to some airy realm where she was free to leave her more serious self behind. Grady, though, just watched her in pleased silence until she had finished. When he spoke at last, his voice was husky with emotion.

"Oh, Lorna, I love to see the sun shining in your eyes. And I love to make you laugh. I could spend the rest of my life making you laugh."

He spoke of laughter, but there was nothing funny in his message. As Lorna stared up at him, she had a sudden sense of recognition, as though she had known this man from the beginning of time. She swayed toward him tremulously until his lips claimed hers and their bodies intertwined. For the second time that day, she was overcome by a clamorous rush of desire; only now she seemed powerless to stop it. She wanted him too much, and he wanted her, too, with an intensity that warmed her to her very core. His big hands molded her to him until she seemed to lose her separate identity. Surely, she must be melting into him, her breasts pressed hard against his chest, her fingers reaching out for his hair, his face, and running to the muscled contours of his shoulders. There was such strength in his body, but how tenderly he used it, even as she felt his heart pound and heard him moan with a kind of anguish.

"Oh, Lorna." His voice was an urgent whisper before his mouth nuzzled her ear, soon traveling to the column of her throat that he branded with quick, hungry kisses. Then his hands were on her breasts, cupping them beneath the thin fabric of her blouse as she arched her back, her nipples growing firm and taut from the sure touch of his finger tips. And all the while something urged her to give herself more completely, some deep inner longing that lay beyond all common sense and ached for surrender.

Yes, surely her body was a gift to give, for she had been promised to him from the beginning of time. Or had she? She fought to clear her mind before she remembered. She barely knew the man. That was the reality of this crazy situation, no matter how tangled her thoughts had become. It was slowly and with a great effort that she managed to pull away from him.

"Grady, please. I'm sorry, but this is all happening so fast. I need some time to catch my breath."

He was silent for a moment, his face still

bearing the signs of unleashed desire. "Does it scare you, Lorna?" he asked at last.

"Yes, I—I think it does." She turned away from him, suddenly overwhelmed by the enormity of her own emotions. They were what frightened her, for in his presence she seemed unable to control them. But why, oh, why? What was it about Grady McGraw that had such power over her, that drew her outside of herself to some strange destination that she had never known before? "You see, we're so different from each other. We want such different things from life and—I just never planned for anything like this to happen, at all."

"You mean with an offbeat character like me, don't you?" His grin was rueful. "Well, maybe it's time that you changed your plans. There's no one better than me who can help you to do it."

What gave him the right to think that he could charge into her life and shake the very foundation on which she stood? Maybe it was the game of football that caused him, even in personal situations, to behave with such an overriding sense of force. But this was no football game, and she wasn't about to let him tackle her to the ground. "Please don't rush me," she told him firmly. "I need some time to think this through and—well, maybe it would be better if we spent a little time apart. Otherwise, I'm afraid that we'll be getting into something that we'll be sorry about later on."

"I doubt that," he said knowingly. "But I won't deny you a little time to yourself. Just tell me how much you need, and then I'll wait. Not that I like to sit on the bench, but I don't imagine that you'll want me to stay there forever."

Lorna grinned back at him wryly, feeling as though she were being granted a reprieve. But she did need one, if only to put some distance between her and the emotional maelstrom that overcame her in this man's presence. She drew a deep breath. "Give me about two weeks, Grady. That isn't such a very long time and—"

"Long enough to get awfully lonesome for someone you care about," he said slowly. A couple of leaves, as burnished as the brilliant hair on his head, drifted to the ground, and as she gazed into the depths of his eyes, she felt a sudden sense of remorse. Yes, her two-week reprieve was wise and necessary, but suddenly it seemed to loom before her like some vast desert that she would have to travel alone.

Chapter Six

Nevertheless, Lorna refused to regard her time without Grady as a period of mourning. That wasn't its purpose. It was meant to serve as a sensible opportunity, a chance for her to get her thoughts in order so that she would not be carried headlong into a situation from which there could be no return. And if she kept herself occupied, she was likely to find that she did not even miss him. After all, she had been a whole and self-sufficient person until he had come into her life, so there was no reason to think that things should be different now. When the two weeks had passed, her temporary fever would be gone completely. Then, in a calm and rational frame of mind, she would be able to see the situation for what it was: an improbable, impossible romance that surely had never been meant to last.

That, at any rate, was the advice that Lorna repeatedly gave herself. Still, it proved to be difficult to follow in the days that passed, although not for lack of trying on her part. Determined to fill her time to the brim, she spent extra hours at work, where her efforts actually won her approval from her boss, Roger Haskell. Never openly enthusiastic about anything, it seemed, the aloof Roger was more cordial than he had been at first, even singling her out for praise at a recent staff meeting. "Miss Lambert's fashion expertise has benefited the *Courier*," he explained dryly. "This is precisely the kind of specialized journalism that will go a long way toward improving the newspaper's image." That had been followed by a somewhat more personal message after the meeting had ended. "Keep up the good work, Lorna," Roger had told her, the ghost of a smile barely disturbing the smooth, even features of his handsome face. And although Lorna could not be sure, she thought that she had seen a faint hint of masculine appreciation in his eyes as he had looked at her. Which was very nice, of course; maybe even promising. Oddly enough, though, Lorna found that his change in attitude did not seem to matter. Whenever she saw him, in fact, she was struck by the notion that he was bloodless and that his veins were filled instead with some artificial substance. That was a ridiculous idea; only she could not seem to shake it any more than she could refrain from comparing him with Grady McGraw, who seemed his direct opposite in every way.

Inevitably, and without conscious effort on her

part, her thoughts turned back to Grady. He was on her mind too much, far more than he should be during that two-week period of time when she wanted only to forget him. But if he was not with her in body, he remained so in spirit, and when each evening arrived, she was let down by a feeling of disappointment. How she would have liked to share the experiences of her day with him, laughing as freely and as openly as only he could make her do.

At least the weekend would give her a chance to see him again. Not in person—only one week had passed since she had last seen him—but on his TV show, "North Carolina Replay." Even so, the program was not aired until midafternoon on Sunday, causing Lorna to wonder listlessly how she might fill her hours in the meantime. She must not, of course, allow herself to pine away idly in the quiet rooms of her apartment. She would have to keep busy, and when Sunday morning arrived, Lorna deliberately began to tackle a wallpapering project that she had postponed for far too long.

Although it was a messy task, it proved to be quickly rewarding. She was able to hang the first roll in a matter of minutes, and when she stepped back to survey her efforts, she was highly pleased. The subtly striped pattern of blue and yellow gave her small living room a feeling of tasteful elegance, while it harmonized perfectly with her furniture—a dainty lemon-colored love seat and two ornate blue wicker chairs. They had looked nearly lost against the uncovered white wall, but suddenly they became more defined, brightening considerably as though they had found a real home. Lorna brightened, too, as she continued her work. It satisfied her deeply to know that her sense of color and design was not limited to fashion alone. Her good taste could be used to transform her surroundings as well.

As absorbed as she was in her task, though, she did not forget to check the time. And when three o'clock arrived, she promptly put interior decorating aside, leaving it eagerly for a TV program on a subject that did not interest her at all.

It was not football, of course, that caused something in her heart to turn over as she watched the screen. It was the sight of Grady McGraw, his face on the screen as rough-hewn and as filled with signs of ready humor as it was in person. That day, however, she saw a far different side of him than he had ever shown to her. Although he was relaxed and pleasant for his TV audience, he was, nevertheless, so keenly immersed in a discussion of complex football strategies that Lorna could barely comprehend a word he said. She tried hard enough, her face puckered in concentration, but when he launched into an analysis of the previous day's game, using terms like "bootleg" and "halfback option," she was lost completely. Football, after all, was his life's work, and he spoke of the victory over Drew State with the zest of a military commander who had just triumphed in battle.

Which was true in a way, Lorna knew, but even so, she almost resented the fact that he was so completely absorbed in it. How could she ever hope to find a real place for herself in his world?

There was nothing about it that held meaning for her, while it was plain to see that her interests meant nothing to him. Lorna frowned as the camera cut from a replay of the game and focused again on Coach Grady McGraw. He was attired, she saw, in his favorite sweatshirt and khakis, a familiar-enough uniform that he evidently felt was appropriate for even his appearance on TV. Lorna sighed in frustration when she thought of how much more presentable he would have looked in the clothes that she had chosen for him. What a lost cause that had been! He probably hadn't yet removed them from their boxes, nor, she thought wryly, was he likely to do so in the span of the next decade.

What, then, was it about the man that still had the power to fascinate her? She searched for some answer as she watched him speak, flicking off the television set when the program was over. It was probably just a strange kind of physical attraction that drew her to him, and her cheeks flamed crimson when she remembered how readily she had responded to his hungry embraces. Oh, she had better keep her distance! The man called Night Train was not the man for her, and any journey to love that she might be tempted to take in his arms would be ill-fated, unwise and all wrong. She had to put him out of her mind for good.

When she arrived at the office on Monday morning, she was almost relieved to discover that Roger Haskell seemed the likeliest person to help her to do so. Although her brief meeting in Roger's office was as businesslike as usual, her boss apparently had more than mere business on his mind. He broached the subject in a cool, detatched manner.

"There's a dinner dance at Greenhills next Saturday night, Lorna, and I'd like to invite you to be my guest," he remarked. "I don't often mix with the members of my staff on social occasions, but in your case I find no reason not to make a small exception."

As ever, there was something in his impersonal tone that made Lorna feel uncomfortably restrained. Still, his invitation was not one that she could really refuse. For one thing, it was certainly flattering to be asked, representing, as it did, a kind of personal triumph. That, though, was a secret that she would have to keep to herself. There was no need for Roger to know that he had once been her teenage idol. He had been, though, and if for no other reason than that, she looked forward to Saturday night as the culmination of her former dreams and fantasies. Besides, Greenhills, with its well-manicured grounds and elegantly appointed ballroom, was the local country club, the place where the members of Larksborough's social set enjoyed their leisure hours. Lorna had never been asked there before, but on Saturday night, she would be escorted by no less prominent a person than Roger Haskell himself! It wasn't often that dreams came true—even old and faded ones—and this was an opportunity that she could not refuse.

What more fitting chance would she have to forget about Grady McGraw? That was surely the best part of Roger's coolly issued invitation, for it clearly overshadowed anything that Grady would be likely to offer. His idea of a good time, after all, was a trip to Mack and Annie's Diner. And while their shared evening there had been great fun, it could in no way be regarded as a gala event. Lorna was sure that dinner and dancing at the Greenhills Country Club would suit her style far better.

And that it did, she kept telling herself, as she waited for dinner to be served in the club's handsomely decorated banquet room on Saturday night. For one thing, it was a pleasure to really dress up, and Lorna had done so with her usual flair. Not wanting to look fussy or overly anxious to make a good impression, she wore a simple sheath of black chiffon that bared her arms and shoulders and flowed gracefully from the lines of her willowy form. Her blonde hair, swept high upon her head, was severe, but deliberately so, for it emphasized the drama of her chic appearance. At any rate, Roger had been highly approving when he had picked her up at her apartment, his cool gray eyes examining her as though she were a rare and costly object in an art gallery. And when they had arrived at the club, it was clear that her appearance impressed everyone else as well. Not only did the rest of the men take full notice of her, but the other women did, too, although in many cases their admiration was mixed with uneasy signs of envy.

Well, it was flattering to be admired, Lorna reminded herself, especially by a group of people who would not have given her a second glance six years before. Still, she knew none of them very well, including even Roger Haskell, her elegant date, who lounged at her side in a suit of pale gray silk. When the talk at their table turned to the subject of golf, Lorna fell completely silent. She had never had a chance to learn the game, and as a result, she had nothing to say.

But the conversation needed no help from her, especially since Roger's talkative sister, Marietta, began to monopolize it by herself. Since her marriage two years before to the son of a prominent banker, golf had become her grand passion, second only to bridge and gossip, Marietta admitted with a brittle laugh. Lorna watched her thoughtfully. She had known Marietta briefly in high school where she had been one of the most popular girls. Somehow, though, it was obvious that she had changed. Although she was still vivacious and full of high spirits, there were now lines of dissatisfaction on her face and a cutting edge to her words that bordered on sarcasm. Perhaps she was unhappy in her marriage to the soft-spoken Carter Ashby, who sat quietly at her side. Whatever the reason, though, there was something about her adult life that seemed to have disappointed her badly. By the time dinner was served, Marietta had downed three cocktails, and her words were tumbling freely and without restraint.

"This chicken tastes like rubber!" she exclaimed irritably when she sampled the food on her plate. "Can't those idiots in the kitchen manage to do anything right?" Then her glittering eyes fastened themselves on Lorna. "Maybe you could get Mack and Annie Lambert to share some of their recipes with our cook."

It was a comment clearly designed to embarrass Lorna, but as she replied, she felt far more anger than embarrassment. "I don't think that would be possible," she said, facing Marietta squarely. "You see, my parents guard all of their recipes quite carefully. Most of them are old family secrets, and my mother doesn't like to share them with anyone."

Now all faces turned in surprise to the promising new fashion writer for the *Larksborough Courier* who had just admitted to being Mack's and Annie's daughter. Moreover, Lorna's words created an inevitable gap between her and the others, since they were all far removed from such humble origins. The news took a few awkward moments to register, although the subsequent responses from the men were not unkind.

"Well, I never would have guessed," said Carter Ashby with a well-meaning smile. "I must have passed that little diner a hundred times, only I never would have thought you—er, your parents —Well, I just never would have associated you with the place, that's all."

Then Lorna felt Roger's arm encircle her shoulders lightly, almost proudly. "Yes, it's rather remarkable, isn't it? She certainly has come a long way over the years."

Lorna remained silent. Although she had thought the same thing herself many times, she somehow resented Roger for having said it. After all, it couldn't be entirely true. She hadn't come so far, had she, that she was a virtual stranger to her own family? In fact, only the other night she had fully enjoyed herself in their company. That, however, was the night she had been with Grady McGraw, and it rushed back to her in a sudden flow of memories.

Ironically enough, her evening at Greenhills was supposed to help make her forget all about him, but he was with her still, his easy laughter rippling through her awareness and touching some vulnerable spot within her heart. Always, it seemed, she remembered the way he laughed, and even though he often seemed to be laughing at her, it pleased her just the same.

Roger Haskell, however, was far less lenient in his opinion of the man. "There are rules that people of good standing are expected to observe in every community," he commented dryly when the talk at the table turned to Grady's persistently casual mode of dress. "And there's no getting through to him. God knows that Lorna certainly did her best, but he seems to have laughed off her advice, just as he laughs off everything else in his life. Well, as they say, you can lead a horse to water . . ." He paused, shaking his head in exasperation.

"Rules, rules, rules!" exclaimed Marietta spitefully. "I'm so sick of hearing about rules that I could scream. But you don't fool me for a minute, Roger. Ever since McGraw refused to join your precious country club, you've been fretting about like a wounded peacock. You're jealous, that's all, to think that he's probably got better ways to spend his time." Then, because her own glass was empty, she took her husband's and quickly downed its contents. "Let's hear it for Grady McGraw!" she proposed sneeringly to her husband. "There's a man who stands on his own two feet, not like some mealy-mouthed people whom I won't bother to name."

Although poor Carter Ashby remained uncomfortably silent under Marietta's assault, Roger did not. "You're missing the point as usual," he chided her coldly. "I certainly have nothing personal against the man, Marietta, but his refusal to maintain the dress code is needlessly provoking. And it's unfortunate, too. McGraw could go places in the world if he wanted to, instead of settling for a second-rate career at Southern Tech. But, of course, moving up in the world requires a certain willingness to play by the rules, and not just the rules of football." Roger paused, his well-coiffed hair gleaming like pale gold under the dim lights of the room. "For my money, McGraw has reached a dead end. He's sure to stay in the minor leagues, just laughing the rest of his life away."

Lorna felt a small chill run through her as she listened to Roger's words. Yes, laughter was Grady's most enticing charm, but it was possible that he used it as a way of avoiding the more serious matters of life. Or was laughter his real strength, enabling him to deal with all aspects of life in his unique and beguiling fashion? Lorna could not be sure. She only knew that she longed to be with him again, and not in the correct but frosty presence of Roger Haskell.

"Try not to mind my sister, Marietta," he told

her smoothly as he led her in a fox trot on the dance floor. "She doesn't like to be upstaged. And the fact is that you are, without a doubt, the most stunning woman in the club tonight. I want you to know that I'm extraordinarily proud to show you to my friends."

He meant what he said, for as he guided her on the dance floor, it was with the kind of cool and careful handling that he might have used on a fragile piece of china. Lorna smiled politely to acknowledge his compliment, and although it was a joyless smile, she knew that it was all that he required. A real smile would only disturb the perfect symmetry of her even-featured face and spoil its classic lines. She danced on, even as her memory carried her back to another time, another place. "Oh, Lorna, I love to see the sun shining in your eyes," she heard someone say. "And I love to make you laugh. I could spend the rest of my life making you laugh." Suddenly, those were the only words that she could hear, and they repeated themselves again and again, haunting lyrics that were permanently engraved upon her heart.

Chapter Seven

Lorna had boldly marked the following Sunday on her calendar as the day of her parents' chicken barbecue and country-music jamboree. Although she had attended such events for years in a bored and restless frame of mind, she found herself awaiting that one eagerly. It probably would be fun. The food would be good and plentiful, and the music was sure to be lively and full of genuine spirit. These were not the only reasons, however, that made the occasion suddenly seem so worthwhile. It would give her the chance to see Grady McGraw after her long two weeks without him. He had promised to be there, after all, and as Lorna drove along the rutted road that led to Mack and Annie's Diner that Sunday morning, she felt intuitively that he was a man who kept his word.

As a result, she presented a very different picture than she had the previous night at the Greenhills Country Club. She was simply dressed in a pair of faded jeans and a red checkered shirt. It was an outfit that was bound to please Grady, she thought with a smile of anticipation, and her hair would please him even more. At least she hoped it would, for he had never seen it that way before. But it did look nice, unconfined and tumbling to her shoulders in a cascade of golden waves. She had even tied a red ribbon around her head to hold her hair back, a fitting touch, she thought, for a down-home country barbecue. Of course, it would not do for all occasions. Certainly not for the Sunday morning round of golf at the country club to which Roger Haskell had invited her the previous night. She had been relieved to be able to tell him that she had a previous engagement that she simply could not cancel.

Much of her day, though, would involve hours of hard work. Her parents needed all the help they could get in setting things up, and Lorna knew from past experience that she was likely to be put on kitchen duty for a variety of chores. There would be time for other things, though, when evening came and the local fiddlers serenaded the guests beneath a bright harvest moon. Something within Lorna's memory beckoned her invitingly as she pulled into the familiar parking lot of Mack and Annie's Diner. Those evenings had seemed so mundane and interminable to her when she was a child, but she was a child no longer. Maybe that night she would be one among the many couples that paired off together, her face diffused with a soft glow of contentment as she sat close by her partner's side.

She was right about the work. There were endless tasks to be done, and although Lorna's sister, Lucille, had come from nearby Yanceyville to offer her help, her three small children invariably demanded their share of her attention. So, Lorna became her mother's chief assistant, and as the morning turned into afternoon, she was sure that all the cole slaw in the world must have been prepared by her. She had never before made so much of it, but when people began arriving for the barbecue, she was glad that she had. There was quite a crowd already, and attendance promised to become livelier as the time went by. "Are the Rebels here yet?" everyone wanted to know. "We didn't want to miss 'em, so we got here just as early as we could." The members of the team, though, were not due until later, when they would arrive in a group with the coach, Lorna explained patiently as she took people's orders. In the meantime, the spirit of excitement inevitably mounted while customers streamed in, greeting each other gregariously and waiting for the appearance of their favorite local football stars.

"That's them! They finally got here!" exclaimed Lucille's little boy Tim some two hours later as he tore out of the diner with an autograph book in his hands. And sure enough, Lorna saw from her place behind the counter, several carloads of smiling young men now appeared in the parking lot where they were besieged immediately by their fans. Was Grady among them, she wondered anxiously as she took an order from a large family group with several crying babies. If so, she could not see him in the confusion. Nor could she join her nephew Tim by dashing out the door to greet him. She had her work to do, and to judge by the long line of people who were still waiting to place their orders, she would remain behind the counter for hours.

Time wore on before her sister, Lucille, whose two youngest children had been put down for naps, mercifully offered to help her out. "No sense in your hiding behind the counter all day, Lorna Lee, not while there's so many cute fellows outside who might like to spend some time with you." She winked cheerfully. "Run along now and have yourself some fun for a change!"

Lorna gladly took her sister's advice, suddenly feeling like Cinderella on her way to the ball. Not that the jammed picnic tables with their throngs of familiar faces or the smell of barbecued chicken was in any way reminiscent of a ballroom setting. This, after all, was just home ground, as plain and ordinary a place as Lorna had ever known. Nevertheless, the presence of the Rebels touched it with a special glamour that could not be denied.

She moved slowly through the thick of the crowd, her eyes peeled intently for a crown of rust-colored hair that would signal the unique presence of the man largely responsible for the barbecue's success, the only person, in fact, she wanted to see. But he was not among the picnickers, nor was he signing autographs in that throng of players who were encircled by eager little boys. Although Lorna was jostled on every side by people of all sizes, shapes and generations, she had the sinking sense of being all alone. More-over, she felt a knot of anxiety tighten within her. He must be here somewhere, she thought, but what could she possibly say in greeting when she found him? She was the one who had called for time out two weeks before, and now it was she who must make the next move. Under the circum-stances, though, that seemed like a bold and risky thing to have to do. Perhaps he had grown tired of waiting. Worse yet, perhaps he had grown to resent her for putting him off so coolly.

"Over here, Lorna!" she heard a familiar voice cry. "Join the team, why don't you, and we'll give those rascals a real run for their money!"

Before her, on the grassy parcel of land behind the diner, stood Billy Ray Turner with a football in his hands. He was grinning broadly, one among a motley group of players who evidently were trying to enlist others to join them for a ragtag game of touch football. What an unlikely and mismatched bunch of athletes they were, Lorna noted with a smile. The tiny Billy Ray, chipper in a fishing cap and a crazily cartooned T-shirt, looked less ferocious than ever, especially in contrast to the great girth of Uncle Bob Wilkins, a bearded, overalled figure who was filling up on beer in preparation for the next play. Nor was the team devoted exclusively to members of the male sex, Lorna saw, for with them was a bulky woman of about fifty who was as short and solid as she was wide.

"Well, I don't know the first thing about foot-ball; I've never even played before," Lorna re-plied hesistantly. Not that the others looked like experts, of course, but they probably had at least some basic understanding of the rules of the game.

"We don't care; we'll take you, anyway," Billy Ray told her as he drew her amiably into the circle. "The fact of it is that we're behind, so we need all the bodies we can get. Those other guys may think they're hot stuff, but they haven't seen anything yet. We're gonna knock the socks off 'em before we call it a day!"

Lorna looked across the field at the grinning members of the opposing team. The "other guys," however, were as unlikely a bunch of athletes as the ones whom Billy Ray had assembled—all, that is, except for one. Lorna's heart lurched wildly. She could not be mistaken about that red hair and the achingly familiar stance of that tall, vigorous body. No, it was Grady McGraw who stood out from the crowd in his usual way and who surely would be her most dangerous opponent in a game that she had never played before.

Whether or not he noticed her, though, Lorna could not tell, for she caught only the briefest glimpse of him before Billy Ray called for the undivided attention of his teammates. During the next play, he explained in conspiratorial tones, he would snap the ball to Muriel, the hefty lady who wore a rough-and-ready look on her square-jawed face, and she, in turn, would pass it to Uncle Bob.

"But what do you want me to do?" Lorna asked nervously.

"Why don't you just sort of mosey out a little ways to the sideline and wait a while?" Billy Ray suggested sagely. "It looks to me like you'd make a pretty fair safety valve just in case we should run into trouble."

Lorna nodded gravely, not understanding a word he had said. She felt a twinge of relief, though. Whatever a safety valve might be, it didn't sound as if the position would place her in the thick of battle. Billy Ray was probably anxious to see that she merely stayed out of the way, at least until she could pick up a few pointers on the way the game was played.

Before she knew it, one team was facing the other as Grady thankfully remained far away in back of the opposite side of the field. Then the ball was snapped back, and Uncle Bob began puffing ahead as fast as his huge frame would allow, waving his arms and calling with a loud rumble, "Right here, Muriel! Throw 'er to me!" Muriel, though, was blocked on all sides by opposing players, and to make matters more critical, Grady began to charge menacingly in Uncle Bob's direction. With a frowning assessment of this emergency, Muriel responded quickly, aiming the ball to the only unguarded spot on the field. And that was where Lorna stood. It flew toward her with the speed of a bullet, so that she braced herself, stunned beyond belief when she actually caught it against her chest.

"Don't just stand there! Run for it! Run!" came the agitated voices of her teammates. So she did, tearing ahead urgently for several feet until she felt an unidentified man from the other team reach out and grab her shoulders. "Gotcha!" he exclaimed breathlessly.

Although she had been stopped, the progress that she had made was a source of jubilation to her teammates. "That's one tough lady!" and "Keep it up, sugar, and we'll crush those guys into mush!" they shouted boisterously. Lorna was filled with a dizzying surge of pride. It was absurd, of course, to be so overcome by what had been just a crazy streak of beginner's luck, but she couldn't seem to help herself. Nor could she keep her confidence from mounting as Billy Ray explained the next play to his teammates in a state of lively animation.

"Okay, guys, now that we've got 'em good and scared," he growled, "we're gonna fake 'em out." Then he barked out his next orders with such gusto that he might have been a Lilliputian general who was facing the battle of his lifetime. Because Lorna had proved to be so dangerous on the flank, he explained, she was sure to be covered by the opposition on the next play. Instead, the ball would be snapped to Uncle Bob, who would divert the opposition by making a run to the line. Then he would throw a surprise pass to where Lorna had run "down long"—"thataway," Billy Ray said, showing her with a pointed finger—and because it was unlikely that she would be covered by anyone any longer, she would be able to freely carry the ball into enemy territory for a touchdown. Lorna nodded keenly, her eyes narrowed against the bright rays of the October sun. She had become a valuable player, even in her very first game. In the mounting thrill of battle, she wanted very badly to win.

Billy Ray was right, too, she saw, as the play got underway. The other players first began to rush at her, but soon it was Uncle Bob who drew them in. Now she was virtually deserted, it seemed, and she was filled with a surge of power. But as she raced forward to receive Uncle Bob's anticipated pass, she saw that she was not as abandoned as she had first believed. There was someone charging toward her, a strapping red-headed figure who wore a wicked smile on his face.

The ball sped in her direction as her opponent stalked her menacingly, the movements of his big, solid body filled with a sense of single-minded determination.

She dodged him as she kept one eye on the ball. "Look out! You're in my way!" she shouted.

"That's the idea," he returned with an evil grin.

She rushed toward the ball, but he reached it first, batting it away from her with a long arm that she could not possibly match. "You can't do that!" she cried in outrage. "It's for me!"

She lunged forward, and it was then that she collided against him, her body hitting his with a sudden impact that caused them both to lose their balance. Down they tumbled in a sprawling heap on the grass. Lorna landed on top of him, her legs entangled with his, and she looked with astonishment into his vivid pair of blue-green eyes.

"Oh!" she blurted abruptly, too breathless for the moment to say anything more.

Beneath her, though, he smiled with lazy enjoyment, even as she felt his heart beat quickly and steadily, the long, hard length of his body exuding a sense of undaunted energy. "I've run into some tough opposition in my day"—he chuckled in a low, easy tone of voice—"but never anything like you. It could be that I'll never recover."

Lorna laughed in response, slowly at first but building into a cascade of unabashed delight as she continued. She was so caught up in her laughter that for a few moments she forgot that she was still lying on top of him in this unlikely position with all eyes upon her. Then, still laughing, she rolled over onto the grass.

"You know, you show real progress for someone who isn't a football fan," Grady drawled teasingly. "Unless you've had a change of heart."

Although his voice was playful, there was a sense of urgency in his eyes that made him, her most threatening opponent, seem oddly vulnerable. "Well, I've missed you, Grady," Lorna heard herself say, her words tumbling from her mouth of their own accord. "I've missed you so much that I thought these past two weeks would never end."

There! If she had wondered what she would say to him, she need wonder no more. She had said it all and on no uncertain terms. Shyly, she turned her face away, not wanting to meet his eyes. His response, however, for which she held her breath, was curiously elusive.

"Well, we can talk about it later," he said in a husky tone of voice. "But not here. We've got a game to play, remember?"

So they did, Lorna realized with a start, and she

returned to her teammates almost dizzily. This time, though, she had far more on her mind than the crazy contest that engaged her, and she was relieved when it ended at sundown in an even draw. "We did okay," Billy Ray chortled as he left the field. "We gave them a run for their money."

His words trailed off in the gathering dusk, and Lorna felt a chill. How much shorter the days were getting now that winter approached, and how much cooler the night breezes felt as they ruffled through her hair! She ambled slowly off the field by herself, aware that Grady, who remained behind, was speaking in a low voice to Uncle Bob, although his words were indistinguishable to her. Well, maybe he didn't want to be with her, after all. Maybe someone else had caught his eye or maybe he had had a change of heart.

Perhaps not though, Lorna thought with a tremor of hope as he caught up with her a few moments later. "The music will be starting soon," he remarked lightly. "We ought to find ourselves a place to sit before—" He stopped suddenly as he pointed to a shooting star that was careening through the dusky sky. "Look at that, will you?" he mused aloud. "I wonder where it's going."

Lorna watched it, a tiny, errant spark of light that seemed to have been freed mysteriously from its place in the heavens, searching, perhaps, for its own special destiny on the earth below. Then she made a wish upon it, not with words but from some secret, unknown sense of longing that nearly made her tremble. For a moment, she followed

the course of the star with unblinking eyes, and
when she turned to Grady, she saw that he
watched it, too, his upturned profile intense with
concentration and touched by a silent sense of
wonder.

After that, the evening flowed along smoothly,
playing itself out before Lorna's eyes like a scene
from an old movie that she had seen a hundred
times before. The country fiddlers were their
usual selves, wrapping their audience in the simple sounds of nostalgic country tunes. As they
played, the sky darkened, and people huddled
together against the approaching chill of night.
There they had found a temporary source of
warmth and comfort in the world that was too
tempting to leave behind. They lingered on, resting against each other's shoulders peacefully,
their occasional voices drifting through the dusky
air like puffs of smoke. Yes, it had always been
like this, Lorna mused dreamily, but even as she
watched it all, she had the sense that she was very
much a part of it, too.

Once, of course, she had been a detached
observer, noting each and every shortcoming of
such events with a sharply critical eye. The musicians, after all, her father undeniably included,
were the rankest of amateurs, while the facilities
of Mack and Annie's Diner were as plain and
ordinary as they could be. All of those things
were still true, but as she sat by Grady's side, they
barely seemed to matter. It was his nearness that
touched the scene with a kind of magic, while the
solid warmth from his body was a miracle that she
wanted to savor.

It was growing late, though, and the evening could not last forever. In fact, some people were leaving already, carrying sleeping children in their arms. Lorna sighed under her breath. She would have to stop by the kitchen to help her mother put things away. Then she, too, would have to be on her way. Under the circumstances, though, she would have to leave alone. Not that she wanted to, but since she had come in her car and Grady had come in his, there seemed to be no other choice.

Grady, though, obligingly waited for her to finish her chores in the kitchen, and afterward she was secretly pleased to find that he had a different idea for the rest of the evening. "Look, Lorna, I don't live too far away," he told her softly as the musicians began to pack their instruments in cases. "Why don't you follow me to my place so we can talk for a while?" His eyes held hers intensely, even as his mouth slipped into a warm and engaging grin. "Besides, I serve a mean cup of coffee, not to mention the cheese and crackers. You can't afford to miss those; they're the specialty of the house."

She could not take her eyes from his as she replied. "Yes, Grady, I'd like that very much." It was not the thought of coffee, though, that sent the blood racing through her veins and caused her knees to weaken. It was the sure knowledge that they would be alone together. So she had not lost him, after all!

Soon Lorna was in her car, following his jeep along a narrow road that led to a chain of small lakes that were popular with local fisherman. It

was a sparsely populated area containing only
infrequent houses that faced the water and rustic
cabins that were well hidden by groves of trees.
Should she really have accepted this invitation,
Lorna wondered, suddenly feeling almost brazen
by following him. But why not? There was nothing amiss in visiting a man's home for coffee, and
there was so much that needed to be said that
night just between the two of them. And besides,
she was curious about Grady's house. He lived
out there year round, he'd said, so it was likely
that he occupied one of the newer homes that had
been built in the past few years. As Lorna drove
farther along, her imagination began to provide a
pleasant picture in her mind. Grady's house
would not be elegant—she was certain of that—
but it was sure to be quite satisfactory, perhaps
one of those modern wood and glass structures
with an open interior and an abundance of win-
dows that overlooked a scenic view of nature.

This image, however, was far from the case. As
Grady pulled off a narrow road to park his jeep,
Lorna was met by a sight for which her imagination had not prepared her. No, she had not
expected glamour, but she certainly hadn't expected anything like what she saw. The man lived
in a one-room log cabin like a virtual pioneer
from days gone by! But he was no pioneer; he was
a former professional football star who surely
could afford more up-to-date and convenient
accommodations. Lorna followed him silently to
the front door. His permanent home, then, was
one of the fishing cabins that were more frequent-

ly used on weekends by local vacationers. Why, though, had he chosen to rough it here all year long, Lorna wondered with a frown, especially when there were so many more desirable places where he could live?

Grady, though, seemed proud of his house as he led her inside and flicked on a light. "It's what you might call cozy," he told her with a pleased smile. Lorna nodded mutely, wondering if she would ever understand this man. Oh, it was certainly cozy; there was no other way that a one-room cabin could possibly be described. Still, as she looked about, she had to admit that it possessed a certain woodsy charm. There was a stone fireplace along one of the roughly textured walls, lined on either side by shelves of books. In front of it sprawled a comfortable-looking sofa and a sturdy brown corduroy chair. Overhead, an arched ceiling gave the room a sense of spaciousness, while the broad, wooden floorboards beneath added to its rustic atmosphere. It was, the perfect spot for a weekend retreat in the woods. To Grady McGraw, however, it was a year-round home.

"That's Paradise Lake out there," he told her as he showed her to a night-darkened window where she was unable to see anything except a rolling expanse of blackness. "Well, it's better in daylight," he admitted with a chuckle. "You'll have to come out someday and see for yourself. There's a terrific view and some of the best fresh-water fishing you could ask for. Maybe that's why they call it 'Paradise,'" he concluded on a note of deep satisfaction. "Anyway, it's the closest place to it that I've ever found in the world."

For a moment, Lorna could only wonder where he had been in his life that caused him to compare this with paradise. Obviously, he had been to far different places than she, for in her eyes there was nothing about the spot that really lifted it above the ordinary. And, most certainly, there was nothing about a one-room cabin, which offered only the most rudimentary kinds of comfort, that struck her as being worthy of pride. She and Grady McGraw had far different notions of heaven, reminding her once again how different they were. Nevertheless, she enjoyed being with him, finding more pleasure in his company than she had ever found with anyone else. It made no sense that he should fill her with such a warm sense of delight, but as she watched him smile at her in his lopsided way, she found that she could not seem to care. For whatever reason, she was glad to be with him, even in a one-room cabin that represented a life-style that she could not understand.

Besides, he possessed a magnanimous gift for hospitality that made her feel instantly welcome. After the coffee began to perk in his tiny kitchenette, he brought out a generous platter of cheese and crackers that he set graciously before his guest. Then, because he wished her to feel "right at home," he took the time to build a fire, lifting several logs from a tall stack on the floor and placing them into the fireplace. Lorna watched him work, his broad-shouldered back turned toward her from her place on the sofa. As ever, there was a sense of forceful, fluid grace in his movements, the sign of a physically active man who could rely on his body to serve the dictates of his will. Lorna turned away to look around the room, and she felt the growing heat of the fire bring a flush to her face. Where in this one-room dwelling, she wondered, was there a place for him to sleep? The sofa she sat on probably converted into a bed. This was such a disconcerting thought though, that she left her seat to join him on the floor in front of the fire.

"It feels good, doesn't it?" he remarked with pleasure, the flames casting a luminous glow on his boldly featured face, highlighting his hair with arresting shades of red and amber. "The first fire of the season is always special." He turned to face her fully, his eyes filled with such concentration that there appeared to be nothing visible in the room but her. "You should always wear your hair that way, Lorna," he said wonderingly. "It reminds me of a sunset on the lake, all gold and shimmering with a thousand lights." He paused, his eyes still fastened on her before he spoke again. "So you've decided that you want to see me again. Maybe you should tell me why."

Lorna's heart skipped a beat, while the crackling of the flames provided the only sound in the quiet room. "Well, I—I like to be with you, Grady," she said after a moment. "But I don't think I can give you a reason. I mean, I just feel good when I'm with you."

"That's promising," he said, grinning, "especially since the feeling is mutual."

Lorna smiled at him warmly. "Yes, but—but doesn't it seem strange? We're so different from each other and—" She broke off, laughing self-consciously as she turned her face away from his penetrating eyes. "There are so many things about you that I don't even understand. Why you live here in a one-room cabin, for example, when you could have so many nice things around you."

"But I already do," he insisted, his eyes never leaving her face.

"That's not—it really isn't what I mean, Grady," she told him in a fluster.

"It's what *I* mean, though." Although he smiled, his voice was firm and low as if he had just uttered a personal creed. "You see, I've got everything in this room that really matters to me, and I've learned the hard way just what that is. Believe me, it has nothing to do with collecting status symbols and hoping they'll fill up your life for you. They can't do that; they never will."

Lorna nodded slowly as she tried to absorb the meaning of his words. "Yes, but don't you think you're overdoing things just a little, Grady? I mean, you don't have to go overboard to prove your point."

He laughed easily, not the least bit disturbed by her comment. "I'm quite content just as I am. Living here suits me very well," he explained as he looked about the room. "Of course, maybe you're thinking that it's too small, but it's big enough for now. There's no reason why I couldn't add on to it if I ever decided to marry again."

Lorna felt something wrench within her. "I

didn't know you were married before, Grady. Was it—was it for a long time?"

"An eternity." He laughed, but even so, she detected a raw edge of pain in his laughter. "At least it seemed that way, but the agony lasted only two years before the divorce was final. It's all over now, so there's no reason to let it spoil our time together."

He didn't want to talk about it, Lorna saw, but even so, she was too curious to leave well enough alone. "Do you have any children?" she asked him guardedly.

His low burst of laughter was incredulous, sounding, too, as though it had sprung from a secret well of sorrow. "No. Nothing good came from that marriage, not even kids." He paused, growing reflective before he reached for her hand. "Look, Lorna, it's a hard thing for me to talk about," he said slowly in a grave attempt to gain her understanding. "I'd like to tell you later, but not just now. Besides, it's all in the past where it belongs. There's still the present and the future, and that's all I care to think about now that you're here by my side."

She felt his hands in her hair, stroking it as though it were made of fine silk, then gathering it in his hands with trembling fingers. "Love is all we need to have in common, Lorna," he murmured tenderly. "So forget about our differences. They'll take care of themselves in time."

As she met his eyes for a fleeting instant, she felt sure that he had foretold a magical future. And when he kissed her lips, it was as though he

were fulfilling some golden promise for which she
had waited all of her life. They belonged together
for all time, it seemed, for whatever reason or
perhaps for none. What difference did it make,
though, when his embrace heated her as intensely
as the blaze of the fire? Her arms pulled him
closer as she kissed him back, glad when his
tongue parted her lips to greet her with an
intimacy that was all consuming. She was lost in
this long moment, no longer a thinking being, but
one who knew only a spinning rush of pleasure.
She leaned her head back as he covered her neck
with kisses, finally stopping at the pulsing hollow
of her throat. "Oh, Lorna," she heard him moan
softly, even as she felt his muscles surge with
desire, his arms pressing her to him with all of
their strength.

They swayed together, and before she knew it,
they were lying together on the floor their faces
dappled by the fire's flickering glow. Grady
reached up with his long arm for a pillow on the
sofa, which he placed beneath her head. Very
slowly, he smoothed out her tumbling hair on it,
and when he spoke, his voice was an adoring
whisper. "Let me love you, Lorna. I want so
much to love you."

Suddenly, she was afraid, but when his fingers
began to undo the buttons of her shirt, she felt
betrayed by her own desire. She must stop him, of
course, but how could she when the urgent feel of
his hands on her breasts had the glorious power to
warm her through and through? Oh, how sweet it
would be to abandon herself completely for the

pleasures of this moment! It was what she longed for, as much as he, and yet those clamoring voices of doubt in her mind had grown far too loud to ignore.

She jerked up abruptly, her hands clutching at her opened blouse. "No, Grady, please. Not now—not like this."

She was aware that his breath, drawn quickly and unevenly, was a sure sign of the desire that still possessed him. Turning away, Lorna was filled with a feeling of shame. Why had she let things go so far? When all was said and done, Grady McGraw was still her direct opposite in every way, a pleasant day at her parents' barbecue notwithstanding. A real future with him would be impossible. So what, then, had brought her to the floor of his log cabin in a moment of such wild abandon? It had been nothing more than lust, she thought remorsefully, a physical urge so raw and powerful that it had almost blotted out everything else in her mind.

But not entirely. She buttoned her shirt quickly before she stood up on shaky legs. "Maybe I'd better go, Grady," she told him, her voice sounding faint and far away. "I—I don't think my coming here was a very good idea."

Then he was on his feet, dominating her with his sheer height, while his hair, rumpled only minutes before by her own hands, glowed brilliantly from the lights of the fire. "You don't have to run away, Lorna," he said with a sigh, and although his voice was quiet, his words were uttered in the tone of a command that could not be disobeyed. "We've got some talking to do, and we might as well do it now." His hand on her wrist was firm, and before she knew it, he had led her to a small table where they faced each other warily, two strangers at once intimate and yet miles apart.

Chapter Eight

It was piping-hot coffee that Grady served in two earthenware mugs that finally broke their awkward silence.

"Suppose you tell me what's on your mind, Lorna," he proposed as the steam from the coffee drifted up through the air.

"Nothing," Lorna told him with embarrassment, careful not to look at him too closely. "At least a few minutes ago I wasn't thinking of anything at all. And that's just the problem. I'm not ready to get so involved. I mean, there are still so many things about this that don't make a whole lot of sense."

"Maybe they aren't supposed to"—he chuckled —"beyond the fact that we seem to care for each other. Anyway, whether you know it or not, I'm good for you, Lorna. You'll have to come down to earth sooner or later, and I'd like to be the one to help you do it. Granted, you may not be there just yet, but you show every sign of making progress. So why not trust me? I've already made the trip myself, and I can get you there in no time."

Night Train was embarked on some strange destination, Lorna thought with irritation, but that did not give him the right to expect her to drop everything in her life and journey with him to the end of the line. Besides, he made her mad when he talked so arrogantly, for it was as if he felt that he possessed some special knowledge that she herself did not. "Grady, I had a good time today," she tried to explain. "It was offbeat and fun, but it—it isn't the way I want to live my whole life. There are lots of other things that are important to me, things that you seem to know and care nothing about."

"Oh, I know about them," he returned with a maddening burst of laughter. "But you are right when you say that I don't care about them. I guess that's what worries you so much. After all, why should you feel anything for a guy who insists on laughing at everything you hold so near and dear? That's the problem, isn't it, Lorna?"

In spite of herself, she felt an irresistible smile steal about the corners of her mouth. "Yes, it is, Grady, and it isn't funny," she replied, struggling valiantly to look as serious as this topic of conversation surely warranted. "Maybe you think appearances are unnecessary, but I don't. They mean a lot to me and—" She broke off on a sigh. "You know, I watched you on TV last week, hoping that our shopping trip would have had some effect on you. But it didn't. I just can't understand you. You have a certain position to maintain, and you persist in meandering about town as if—well, as if you were a workman from the print shop of the newspaper. That's what I thought you were when I first met you."

He nodded, but for once there were no signs of humor in his eyes. They studied her gravely, mesmerizing her with something that seemed to strip her to her very core. "And what if I were, Lorna? Would it have made a difference?"

"That isn't what you are, Grady," she returned hotly, "so that's hardly the point."

"Oh, but it's very much the point. I'm only sorry that you've missed it." He watched her testily. "You know, you may be Mack and Annie's daughter, but you still have a long way to go for yourself. Much further than I might have guessed. In fact, I'm surprised that you've consented to even grace me with your presence tonight. Someone like Roger Haskell, our dearly beloved stuffed shirt in residence, would seem to suit your tastes far better."

Oh, how unsparingly perceptive he could be, so much so that he pried too deeply into a private matter that she didn't wish to share. It was not his reference to Roger himself that seemed too blatantly unfair, for Roger had never meant anything to her in a personal way. Nor would he ever, she realized, as she recalled her evening with him at the country club only the night before. Nevertheless, Roger represented a gracious life-style that she had always envied and admired. What was wrong, after all, with membership in the country club? And what was wrong with enjoying those things of taste and elegance that money alone could buy in this world?

"Roger isn't so bad," she said, reluctantly coming to his defense. "I don't suppose you could ever like him, Grady, but you'll have to admit that he has some good points."

"Name one." This comment was put to her so disbelievingly, so disparagingly, that it provoked her even more.

"Well, he cares about how he looks, for one thing," she retorted. "Maybe it's because he takes his position in life seriously instead of laughing at it as if it were some kind of great big joke."

"That, I take it, applies to me." He was angry now, angrier than Lorna had ever seen him before. She was not surprised, however, for she had sensed this quality in him on the day of their first meeting. It was nothing less than a capacity for wrath that was as fierce and raging as a thunderstorm at sea. And although the thought of somehow taking shelter from it was tempting, he had given her no place to hide.

"Well, doesn't it apply, Grady?" she shot back, determined to weather the inevitable storm as bravely as she could.

"You'd never ask that question if you knew me," he told her, his whole being tensed with quiet but gathering fury. "And since you won't trouble yourself to look beneath the surface, then why should I trouble myself with you? At this moment, in fact, you remind me far too much of

Pat, my former wife. She was concerned about my position in life, too, all for the sake of my own good, of course. She married me when I was at the top of my career in pro ball, and she saw to it that we were surrounded by every status symbol in the book. Then she divorced me two years later when I was flat on my back from an injury that forced me out of the game for keeps. No more lofty position, no more sweet and loving Pat." He laughed bitterly, and his unsmiling eyes scrutinized Lorna without mercy. "So don't try and change me. You won't do it. I've come to look at people for what they are underneath, and I expect them to do the same for me. Those are my terms, Lorna; I need a woman who can live by them, too. From what you've told me about yourself tonight, you're not even willing to try."

Lorna said nothing, so chastised by his words that she felt dangerously close to tears. How could he compare her to his ex-wife, implying that she, too, was capable of using him in such a way? She would never resort to such cruelty, never in all her life. He was being grossly unfair to imply that she would! Yes, of course she valued many of the luxuries that went with money and prestige, but that was only because she had never had them as a child. The same was not true of Grady, however, another reminder to her of how vastly different they were. Perhaps those differences could never be bridged.

She drew a deep breath, struggling to speak against the lump that had risen painfully in her throat. "You've got no right to hurt me this way, because you don't understand me anymore than I understand you." She rose wearily from the table, noting without interest that her coffee had grown cold. Not nearly as cold, however, as the fierce man who sat across from her and who, only moments before, had wanted to love her with such heated desire. "I'm leaving now, Grady. It's late, and I guess—well, it looks like we both have a lot of things to think over."

"To say the least," he affirmed cryptically as he began to lead her to the door. And when he bid her goodnight, it was as impersonally, as if she had been peddling a product for which he had no earthly use. "Be careful when you turn around on that road," he instructed her curtly. "There's a ditch alongside of it."

She nodded, stepping outside as a great well of emptiness began to ache within her. He probably didn't want to see her again; when he began to offer his final words of parting, she felt certain of it. "Look, I've got a busy week coming up, so don't expect to see me for a while. Unless, of course, you decide to break one of your rules by coming to my game on Saturday. There's a little more to it than our game of touch football this afternoon, but maybe you don't want to find out that for yourself. That would mean meeting me halfway, except you've never shown me any signs that you were willing to make the effort."

Was that an invitation to his game, or was it merely a disparaging comment on her lack of interest in his work? Lorna could not tell. It was true, though, that she had never attended a single game at Southern Tech. There were always dozens of other things that had always taken priority. She had set aside the following Saturday, in fact, as an opportune time to shop for a new winter coat. The shopping trip could be postponed, however, especially if Grady was really sincere about wanting her to attend his game. Still, he said nothing more, impatient, perhaps, that she be on her way.

"Well, I'll see what I can do, Grady," she said uncertainly. His response was to shut the door, leaving her to stare at it dejectedly. Was it really all over between them, or could they somehow manage a new, if not somewhat shaky, beginning?

If the moon above had any answers, it guarded them elusively. Lorna stared at it for a long moment, a pale ball of ivory that seemed to be gazing back at her from over the night-blackened waters of Paradise Lake. A chill shook her, and she turned to walk to her car.

"Looks like the boss has a trick up his sleeve," muttered Billy Ray Turner in a disgruntled tone of voice as he showed Lorna a memorandum that Roger had written to all members of his editorial staff. Looking up from the pile of work on her desk, Lorna perused it quickly.

"I don't think so," she reassured Billy Ray with a smile. Certainly, the contents of the memo seemed routine enough to her. It was necessary, Roger explained, that the files in the personnel department be brought up-to-date in the interests of "good housekeeping." As a result, he was requesting his employees to turn in copies of their transcripts so that their educational backgrounds would be thoroughly documented. "I know it's a nuisance to have to write away for transcripts," Lorna conceded, "but most employers do require it these days."

"Well, I don't like the looks of it," Billy Ray fretted uneasily. "Even if I had a fancy transcript from Harvard to wave in his face, I don't see what difference it would make. Fact is, I've been doing my job for thirty long years and—"

"Roger knows that, Billy Ray. Everyone knows how valuable you are around here. All of the formal schooling in the world couldn't take the place of what you've learned from experience," she said with heartfelt certainty as she handed him back the memo. "So you don't have a thing to worry about. This is just Roger's way of keeping records. Besides, he probably wants to impress us with how much he learned in business management school," she concluded with a giggle.

Billy Ray brightened. "Maybe so. I keep having to remind myself that times and generations change, but that's what happens when you get to be as old as I am." Tucking the memo in his pocket, he turned toward his cubbyhole office, which was only a few feet away.

"Billy Ray, wait!" Lorna called on a sudden impulse. "Do you know if there are any tickets available for this Saturday's game? I know it's a last-minute request, but—well, if there's any chance that I could go, I'd really like to." Billy Ray knew everyone in town, and if anyone could wangle a football ticket at this late date, Lorna knew, then surely it was he.

"That so?" he replied perkily. "I guess maybe our game on Sunday really whetted your appetite. Or maybe it was the coach himself who had something to do with making a fan out of you," he suggested with a sly chuckle. "That man really works wonders on young people, wouldn't you say?"

Lorna dodged the question by saying nothing even as a surge of color rushed to her face. Yes, the man had worked a certain kind of wonder on her, and she badly wanted to see him again, if only to show him that his worst suspicions of her were wrong. She was not as fixed in her ways as he seemed to believe, nor was she opposed to meeting him halfway as he had apparently suggested. At least it seemed to her now that he had suggested such an arrangement, although she really could not be sure. But she would never find out unless she attended his game, and she had the sinking sense that if she failed to do so, he would slip from her life forever. It was a risk, perhaps, but it was one that she would have to take.

Luckily for her, Billy Ray was more than accommodating. Since he would be covering Saturday's game as an especially welcome newspaper assignment, he invited Lorna to watch it with him in the press box where she would have an overhead view of the entire event. It sounded like fun, Lorna thought with mounting anticipation, and as

the week went by, she found that it never left her
mind at all. There was no reason for her to
dismiss football completely from her life. Surely,
there were things about it that could hold her
interest, and in that respect alone, she supposed
that she still had a long way to go for herself. How
odd, indeed, to think that her journey with Night
Train, whatever its final destination, was filled
with such a sense of discovery and so many
surprises!

Instead of dawning bright and clear, the Saturday of the game began in a gray drizzle of rain.
But no matter, Lorna told herself brightly. The
game would go on as scheduled, while she, from
her vantage point in the press box, would be fully
protected from the weather. So she dressed with
little concern for the rain, wanting to appear as
well put together as the occasion required. She
knew that many people in town, women especially, attended the games in the latest fall styles, so
that she, in her position as the local fashion
adviser, could not afford to neglect her own
appearance. Not that she would have wished to in
any case.

She loved the fashions that year, and as she
checked herself in the mirror, she was more than
pleased. Her new tweed jacket was a soft and
dusky shade of mauve, and because it was stylishly short, it showed off the gathered fullness of the
trousers, which narrowed so appealingly at her
ankles. She also wore a ribbed sweater of deep
violet, which made a daring but successful complement to her blazer, while a delicate necklace of

silver chains added a finishing touch to the whole ensemble. She presented as chic a picture as ever, although once again she had let her hair fall freely to her shoulders. "You should always wear your hair that way, Lorna," Grady had told her. "It reminds me of a sunset on the lake, all gold and shimmering with a thousand lights." She had not forgotten those words; they had stayed with her vividly all during her long week without him.

Later that day, Lorna found herself taking in the pregame spectacle at the stadium as though she were a child on her first trip to the circus. What a colorful pageant it was—the acrobats from the college gymnastic team who entertained the crowd with tumbling feats, the uniformed members of the marching band whose brassy music resounded boldly through the crisp autumn air and the multitude of banners and pompons that waved brilliantly from the stands below. In that respect, at least, football was a treat for the eye, and Lorna found herself eagerly awaiting the contest ahead. It was an important one, too, for many people were saying that if the Rebels won the game, they would have an excellent chance to become the champions of the Southern Mountain States League, the group of small college teams to which they belonged. There might be bigger, more prestigious championships, but few people in the stadium today seemed to know or care. The Rebels were heroes enough for them, and Grady McGraw, who had coached them so successfully up until then, could surely lead them through this crucial victory.

Grady was a man of singular importance in Larksborough that day, and Lorna studied him closely as he stalked along the sides of the grid-iron, following each successive play of his team. There was far more to coaching than Lorna had ever realized; in fact, she felt embarrassed to think of how much she had to learn. Still, she could tell that Grady played many key roles on the field, and it was he to whom every Rebel and assistant coach turned for all of their cues. Not only was he a leader, but also he was a coordinator of strategies so technical and so subject to last-minute change that Lorna could only marvel at his ability to remain clearheaded under such pressure.

The competition from Calvert State proved fierce, while the events of the game occurred in bursts of speed so sudden that it was difficult for Lorna really to comprehend them. She wanted to very much, but her untrained eye could not seem to take everything in. Thankfully, Billy Ray, when his excitement did not get the best of him, made an obliging teacher.

"Watch this next play now," he told her during the second quarter when the score had reached a climactic tie. "Grady's going to try and fake 'em out just like we did the other day at the barbecue. So keep your eye on the flanker, number twenty-eight, 'cause he's the one who'll be waiting for the surprise pass."

Number twenty-eight, however, a freshman Rebel named Hinchley, did not wait long enough but panicked instead. He was on the wrong side of the field when the pass was finally thrown, so that Calvert State gained control of the ball. Jeers and catcalls emanated from the stands as Hinchley, dejected, walked off the field by himself.

Lorna watched the new player sympathetically. Underneath all of that bulky padding, he was just a kid who was crushed for having let down his team at such a decisive moment. And how would Grady react, she wondered anxiously, now that his play had been so badly mangled?

She did not have to wonder for long. Soon Grady had joined the young player, and with an arm about him, he began to speak to him in a confidential manner. Whatever he said must have been positive, Lorna surmised, for Hinchley squared his shoulders and even smiled. Later on, when he returned to the field, he was able to play with renewed confidence, a sure sign of his coach's faith and encouragement. Yes, Grady was many things on the field, Lorna realized with a rush of admiration, for here, as in other endeavors, he rose above pettiness to become a source of benevolent strength to all the people who came into his life.

Lorna's eyes filled with sudden tears as she continued to watch him. Dressed in his usual sweatshirt and khakis, a visored cap covering his arresting head of hair, he probably would never fit the image that she had kept in her mind for so long. But was that really so important? He possessed other qualities, instead, those that had the undeniable power to warm her like sunlight.

Surely, then, it was vital that she learn to meet

him halfway. For the time being, though, there seemed no more opportune way to do so than by keeping her eye peeled on the plays of his game. Afterward, perhaps, she could discuss it with him, possibly impressing him with a few wise comments and carefully made observations. Why let him believe, after all, that she was not capable of meeting him on his own ground? She would show him that she was!

It was when the game reached its final tense moments, however, that Billy Ray abandoned his role of teacher completely. He went wild instead, along with the rest of the crowd, for now, with only fifteen seconds more to play, the Rebels had their last chance for victory in the form of a field goal. This, then, was the most crucial play of all, and Lorna watched it unblinkingly, not wanting to miss a thing. Why, though, had number 5, McGriggin, whom Billy Ray had described as an unreliable kicker, been selected by Grady to kick the ball? Lorna bit her lip, while beside her Billy Ray was bellowing something that sounded like "Boot it, toot it, go, go, go!"

And then everything happened at such full blast that all Lorna could make out was a hurly-burly scramble of bodies. Who was doing what, and where was the ball? Ah, but there it was, she saw with a shining sense of jubilation. McGriggin must have done his job perfectly, for now the ball was traveling into the end zone where it was caught by a waiting Rebel for the game's winning touchdown.

Billy Ray's shouts had become unintelligible, while Lorna celebrated in a quieter way by beaming from ear to ear. Soon enough, though, she retrieved a mirrored compact from her purse for a hasty peek at her appearance. In just a short time, she would be accompanying Billy Ray down to the field, but she didn't want to risk seeing Grady unless she looked her best. Although she had been told many times that she was beautiful, it was something she could never quite believe. Besides, even if it were true she felt a constant need for self-improvement. She applied a fresh coat of lipstick—the rest of her makeup had held up well—and brushed the few stray tendrils of her long hair into place. Then she left the press box with Billy Ray to offer her congratulations to Coach Grady McGraw.

Although he was surrounded by a host of noisy fans and grinning players, she was relieved when he singled her out with an interested gaze.

"I'll bet you just got here," he teased. "I can hardly believe that you gave up a whole Saturday afternoon to watch a boring game of football."

"It wasn't boring, Grady," she said earnestly, knowing that she would have to convince him that she meant what she said. "I enjoyed every minute of it, especially at the end. I was worried about McGriggin, but he—he really came through in the clutch," she added, trying to pick up some of the lingo that was being bantered all about her.

At this, Grady burst into an incredulous burst

of laughter. "Then you must have just gotten here because McGriggin didn't have a thing to do with it. He made a fake kick, and that's what fooled the opposition." Then he shook his head, his eyes full of snapping lights of humor. "I can see that you know as much about football as I do about fashion. Maybe we'll never manage to find that common meeting ground between us."

"Yes, we will, Grady," she heard herself whisper in a tone of tremulous hope. "I mean—well, at least, I think we should try."

"Do you, Lorna?" he asked coolly, and her heart stood still as she waited for him to break the long silence that followed. Then his face softened, while the corners of his mouth tensed with something both tender and full of pain. "Well, since I haven't been able to get you out of my mind all week long, I don't know what else to do but to keep on trying. Look, there's a team party coming up at Mickey's Place in just a while," he added as he began to assess her outfit with shrewd appraisal. "Maybe you'd like to come along. It won't be anything fancy, mind you, in case you were wondering."

"No, I—I didn't think it would be," she replied with a nervous smile. Mickey's Place was just a local pizzeria, but if she found that she was overdressed, she could remove her jacket or even her jewelry, if it seemed necessary. "But I'd like to go just the same." Suddenly, she felt a telltale surge of color redden her cheeks. If only he wouldn't look at her quite that way, his eyes cutting through her layers of clothing to the vulnerable flesh that lay beneath!

"Why don't you meet me outside the locker room in, say, about half an hour?" he proposed with a sudden glance at his wrist watch. "That way we can go to the party together." Then he rewarded her with a full and utterly heart-warming grin. "We'll have fun, Lorna. At least we'll give it another try, won't we?"

Then he was overtaken by one of his assistant coaches, who, holding an official-looking chart in his hands, began to barrage him with questions about the following week's practice schedule. Lorna stepped away, even as a low rumble of thunder sounded from the sky. Not that it bothered her. She was in far too glowing a mood to let the possibility of rain get her down. Besides, it hadn't rained since the early morning, and then there had only been a light drizzle. Yes, the sky was overcast, but it might just as well be streaming with sunshine as far as Lorna was concerned. She was going to be with Grady again! At this promising moment, it was all that really seemed to matter.

As she neared the locker room, though, she was aware that large raindrops had begun to fall. Still, they fell slowly, an encouraging sign that they might go away almost as soon as they had started. At least Lorna hoped they would. There was no place outside the locker room where she could find shelter from a downpour. Nor could she take refuge in her car, for she hadn't even brought it. Billy Ray, who was now inside the locker room, had driven her there instead, and because he had to interview some of the players, it was not likely that he would appear for quite some time.

Another clap of thunder boomed ominously before the rain began to fall in earnest. It hit the pavement with driving force, obscuring everything in sight like a vast gray sheet and splattering on Lorna without mercy. She looked about frantically. She couldn't just wait there like a sitting duck, but what were her choices? Her hasty attempt to get inside the locker room—surely there must be some sort of waiting room in there—was met by a soundly locked door, while the roof of the building had no protective overhang at all. By that time, though, the rain had done its damage. She was drenched, her hair clinging to her face in forlorn, wet tendrils, her soaked clothing hanging shapelessly from her shivering body. Even the lovely colors of her sweater and jacket had darkened beyond recognition in the downpour, while her shoes were so filled with water that her feet slid and slipped whenever she tried to move. And her face—her poor face!—that must be the worst disaster of all, she realized with a sinking heart. Surely, her mascara and liner had run to form dark smudges under her eyes, while the rest of her makeup was probably swimming in unsightly rivulets down her cheeks and neck.

Her teeth chattered as she vainly tried to warm herself by wrapping her arms against her chest. From a distance, she could make out a group of people who were fleeing for the sanctuary of an adjacent campus building that apparently was unlocked. Lorna, though, remained where she was. She was waiting for someone very dear to her, and she did not want to take the chance of missing him. She would simply stay there where she had agreed to meet him until he finally arrived.

Chapter Nine

When the locker-room door finally burst open, Lorna was relieved to see a robust group of players emerge, followed by the stalwart figure of Grady McGraw.

"Let's make a dash for it!" shouted one of the players as the rain beat down on his head. Then he darted off in the direction of the parking lot, joined by his teammates for a laughing, boisterous scramble through the downpour.

Grady, though, took more time to look about him than did his players. "My God, Lorna, how long have you been waiting out here like this?" he asked without waiting for an answer as he wrapped his arm quickly around her. "Why didn't you come inside?"

"I—t-tried, Grady, but the d-door was llocked," she managed to reply through chattering teeth.

"Damn," he muttered. "I should have had the attendant keep it open, but I didn't know that it would start to rain like this." He drew her close to the comforting warmth of his big, well-muscled body and searched her face with concern. "I'm really sorry. And now just look at you!"

She was almost tempted to turn away, for she didn't want to have him see her that way, her hair flattened to her head, the last traces of her makeup running ludicrously down her cheeks. He had already seen the worst, though, so there was no use in hiding or even trying to conceal her feelings. That she had stayed there was positive proof of how much she wanted to be with him. "Well, I d-didn't want to miss you, G-Grady," she admitted with a miserable shiver as she hugged her arms tightly to her chest. "But I g-guess I look like a d-drowned rat, d-don't I?" She made a poor attempt at laughter while her shoulders shook and her teeth continued to chatter from the cold.

"No, you don't," he murmured as he steadied her in the shelter of his arm. She looked up at him in surprise, but for once she saw that he was fully serious. "Oh, Lorna, you're the most beautiful sight I've ever seen."

For a second, she forgot everything else, even the driving rain. There was only Grady, whose blue eyes held her transfixed with their tenderness and whose words surely represented the sweetest, most unexpected compliment that she had ever received in her life. Then they were off and running toward his jeep in the parking lot, laughing in spite of the rain as their feet splashed through the puddles that lay in their path.

It was a blessing to be inside the jeep, a dry refuge from the rain that splattered loudly on the car's roof. Nevertheless, Lorna was overcome by another fit of shivering. Not only were her clothes sopping wet, but also she felt chilled to the very bone.

"I'm going to get you right home," Grady said determinedly as he started the engine and turned the heater to high. "I want you to get dry and comfortable before you change for the party." His hand reached for hers and squeezed it. "Move closer to me, why don't you? I'm not as wet as you are."

"But I don't want to d-drown you," she protested with a faint laugh as she remained where she was. The water from her body had already drenched the upholstery and had gathered at her feet to form a small pool. "J-just d-drive, Grady, and g-get me home as fast as you c-can."

He obliged her by maneuvering the jeep as quickly through the downpour as he was able, and when the heater began to do its work, Lorna felt herself relax. At least she stopped shivering. Far pleasanter things lay ahead, and she was looking forward to them.

"The party will be a victory celebration, won't it?" she asked Grady with a smile, wanting to share in the pride and pleasure of his recent accomplishment.

He nodded with a grin, even as he kept his eyes

on the road. "I guess it's also going to be a sort of surprise birthday party for me," he admitted with a trace of sheepishness. "Except that it won't be a surprise, since I overheard the boys talking about it in the locker room. But we'll have to act surprised, won't we, Lorna, so that we won't let them down."

She agreed cheerfully. "That's really nice of them, Grady," she added with appreciation. "I just wish I'd known it was your birthday, too."

"Well, it's not until Tuesday," he chuckled good-naturedly. "The boys are rushing things a bit, but I won't hold it against them." He had reached her apartment building, and he pulled up directly in front of the door. "Are you prepared for another mad dash through the rain?" he asked her with a wink.

Soon enough and not too much the worse for their latest exposure to the weather, they stood in her small living room, both of them damp and cold. How good to be inside this cozy space, Lorna thought thankfully. She turned to Grady with a glad smile. "Please let me get you a towel or something so that—"

She stopped, for he was slowly enfolding her in his arms. They were alone together, she realized, and the nearness of his body and the clean, brisk scent of him caused her senses to throb with sudden longing. "I know a better way to get warm," he said, his lips brushing her hair and nuzzling her damp face. "Oh, Lorna, my beautiful Lorna, who waited for me out in the rain. I've wanted you so much."

At those words, she felt a sudden surge of

emotion before he kissed her fully on the lips. And yes, oh yes, he was right! There could be no better way than this to forget the bone-chilling discomfort that the rain had caused. His mouth was so warm, so ardently tender, and the heat from his body seemed to engulf her in waves. For a while, they stood pressed tightly together, their arms seeking one another, their lips moving in an urgent quest.

Then his hands began to massage her very slowly and firmly, working from her back and falling to her waist and hips as though he would leave no part of her untouched. Desire flowed through her, all the sweeter for the sense of comfort that she felt from his hands. They moved so surely, so rhythmically, over her that she found herself swaying in response, her lower body engaged in a slow dance that seemed to keep time to something that pulsed within her. Or perhaps it came from him, from the strong, steady beat of his heart that hammered against her breast.

He began to slip her wet jacket from her shoulders. "You won't need this anymore," he murmured huskily. Then he removed it from her arms completely and tossed it without concern to the carpeted floor below.

"Grady, what are you doing?" she managed to ask in breathless surprise.

"I'm warming you up," he returned with a slow smile, "and getting rid of everything that stands in our way." She felt him unclasp her necklace, his fingers working with unexpected delicacy before he added it to the discarded jacket that lay at his feet. "It's not your clothes that make you beautiful to me, so they serve no purpose now. It's the woman underneath that I want to love." Desire made his voice all the deeper, and although his words were spoken tenderly, there was a strong undercurrent of urgency in them as well.

For a moment, Lorna felt herself go limp, giving way to the new wave of longing that coursed through her. How easy it would be to simply give herself up to it and to turn to him as willingly as she would turn to the rays of the sun after a long and chilling winter. Like the sun, he was a source of radiant warmth that could be nearly blinding. She need only offer herself to him as the heat from his body spread into hers, gliding exquisitely through her veins like golden honey. Yes, he had been true to his promise, for the misery of the rain was forgotten. He had burned it away with the sheer force of desire, and when he removed her damp sweater from her body, she could not stop him. She could only glory in the engulfing warmth of his hands upon her breasts.

Soon he began to fondle them more hungrily, reaching under her bra to stroke her nipples with deft fingers, even as he claimed her lips in a kiss that seemed to have no end. Lorna heard herself moan as she swayed against him. Oh, this was good—she craved it so much—and when the tips of her breasts budded fully in response to his touch, she felt wildly intoxicated by her own desire.

Then he began to unclasp her bra, still another layer of wet clothing that he would add to the heap on the floor. Nor would he stop until he had removed everything she wore, for he had said he

wanted nothing to stand in their way. And then—
oh, then there would be no turning back!

Lorna stepped away, dizzy and shaken.
"Grady, no. We've gone too far already and—"
She reached behind her to awkwardly fasten her
bra. "I don't think I'd feel right if I kept the guest
of honor from attending his own party," she said
breathlessly.

"Don't worry about that," he told her as he
drew her possessively into his arms again. "We
can both be a little late."

A wry grin touched her face as she gazed down
at the heap of her discarded clothing. "If we keep
on like this, I'm afraid we'll be more than a little
late. We'll never manage to get there at all."

A strand of his copper-colored hair had fallen
rakishly onto his broad forehead, and he chuckled
with amusement. "You've got me there, Lorna.
We wouldn't make it, would we? We'd just be
keeping all of those good people waiting for
nothing." Then he shifted his stance and sighed
deeply. "Still, you can't keep *us* waiting forever,
you know. There's too much between us that feels
like love, and it's been growing stronger all the
time." He smiled intriguingly, and his eyes locked
with hers, "I thought that maybe you'd noticed it,
too."

Oh, yes, she had surely noticed it, but it was
such an overwhelming thought that she did not
know how to handle it. Love was an emotion so
powerful that it bound two people together for a
lifetime. And yet was she really ready, when all
was said and done, to share the rest of her life

with Grady McGraw? She simply did not know, nor could she let herself think about it at this charged moment.

"I—it's time for me to change, Grady," she said as she scooped her wet clothes into her arms. She must hang them up to dry, she counseled herself sternly, before she replaced them in their zippered plastic bags.

Holding them in her arms as if they were a shield, Lorna walked away quickly. At the end of the hallway, she would find time to be alone, however briefly, in the bedroom and bathroom of her small apartment.

The surprise party had been fun in a boisterous, exuberant way, although Lorna was pleased when Grady admitted to wanting another, quieter birthday celebration with just the two of them. On Tuesday, the day of his birthday, she had to keep herself from speeding as she drove to his office in the Athletic Building on Southern Tech's small campus. She had agreed to meet him there after work before dinner at a restaurant of his choice. And that, as likely as not, would be Mack and Annie's Diner, Lorna reminded herself with a smile as she made another effort to reduce her speed. They certainly wouldn't be going to the Ritz, so that her eagerness to begin what was bound to be a perfectly ordinary evening seemed more than a little crazy.

Or did it? And how could she really think that any time she spent with him would be ordinary after what had happened in her apartment the previous Saturday? Even the memory of it had the power to warm her to her very core. And why, at all other times, too, did she always feel so gloriously alive when she was in his company? The only answer that she could think of lay in the message that he had spoken just three days before. "There's too much between us that feels like love, and it's been growing stronger all the time." Her heart lurched suddenly at the memory of those words. Was this love, this feeling that seemed to shine from her every pore and touch everything in her sight with an unearthly kind of glow? It lay far beyond the realm of reason. There was no logic in it, not even a shred of common sense. Nevertheless, it pulled her irresistibly. If this was not love, then what else could it be?

It was with a light heart that Lorna stepped through the corridors of the Athletic Building to Grady's office on the first floor. Clad in a beige knit dress that sleekly flattered her willowy figure, she fairly flew along, even as she had to keep reminding herself that she was still on solid ground. There was, after all, nothing special about her surroundings. The well-worn building, which served as the modest headquarters for the physical recreation of the college's small student body, was merely plain and functional. There was nothing fancy there, just the faint scent of chlorine from the swimming pool, coupled with the unmistakable aroma of disinfectant. Lorna's heels clicked briskly on the tiled floor as she rounded a corner. She passed two blue-jeaned students who were lounging against the wall with cans of pop in their hands before she finally reached the door to Grady's office.

"Just go right in, miss," one of the students called out pleasantly. "The coach's door is always open."

So it was, she discovered with a smile as she stepped inside. And better still was the sight of that brilliant head of red hair, although the owner of it sat with his back toward her, evidently engaged in paper work of some kind.

"Happy birthday," she whispered as her heart beat faster.

He swung around, greeting her with one of his most endearing grins. "I may be an old man of thirty-six, but seeing you makes me feel like I'm just getting started," he said warmly. Then he gestured to a vinyl chair that sat across from him. "Why don't you take a seat for just a minute, Lorna? I'll be finished with this letter in no time."

She did as he suggested, watching his large frame hunched over the typewriter as he hunted and pecked for the right keys. Then she looked about her at his office, a small, uncarpeted room that was as functional as the rest of the building. A series of charts and diagrams had been tacked on its walls, and in one corner stood a large, portable blackboard, dusty with chalk. Lorna turned back to Grady to see that he was still intent upon his typing.

"Don't you have a secretary?" she asked.

"I do, but I have to share her with two other people on the staff," he said uncomplainingly as he removed his letter from the machine. "Not that Margie isn't a real pro, but she's so busy that I don't like to burden her with extra work unless I have to. And in this case, I don't." He smiled as he folded his brief letter neatly and slipped it into an envelope. "I'm getting better and better at this all the time."

Lorna bit her lip. It was good of Grady to be so considerate of his hard-working secretary, of course, but just the same, it would be nice if he had a secretary all to himself. Roger Haskell had two assistants, she seemed to recall, a receptionist who fielded calls from the waiting area outside his door and a secretary who worked with him in the more private quarters of his inner office. But Southern Tech obviously could not afford such amenities, even for as valuable a person as Grady McGraw. It was a shame, Lorna thought, although Grady clearly did not seem to mind.

Then he rose from his desk, his work finished, and reached for his jacket, which had been draped over the blackboard. "We're going to have ourselves a good time tonight, Lorna," he promised. "I'll bet you'll never guess where I—"

He stopped as the phone on his desk began to ring, an unwelcome intrusion in the quiet room. "I really don't have to answer that," he said as if to convince himself. "It's after five o'clock and—"

Lorna smiled as she settled back in her chair. "Maybe you should, Grady. Besides, I don't mind waiting."

He sighed with impatience as he snatched up the receiver and held it to his ear. "McGraw speaking," he barked gruffly. Then his face took on a hint of surprise, as if he recognized the caller, whoever he was, but had not expected to hear from him at that time.

It was apparently someone from football, Lorna surmised from Grady's response, someone whom he had not seen for several years. She listened carefully, trying to fit the remnants of conversation that she could hear into a logical whole. The caller was from Dallas, she concluded, and although Grady spoke to him cordially enough, she saw his face tighten with a kind of cool wariness that she had never seen in him before. As the conversation continued, Lorna sensed that something important, perhaps even momentous, was being discussed. It sounded very much to her as though Grady were being considered for a job, a highly prestigious one at that, with the professional team on which he had formerly played. Her excitement mounted, and when Grady bid the caller good-by, she was fairly overcome by it.

"Grady, was that what I think it was?" she asked with shining eyes. "I mean, it sounded like the Dallas Cyclones are just about ready to offer you a job!"

"I'm afraid so," he replied dryly as he stared at the telephone. "At least they want to talk to me about coaching the team." He looked toward her, his face marked with undeniable pride but touched, too, with a strange guardedness that Lorna could not understand.

But maybe she was just misinterpreting it. This

was wonderful news, holding, as it did, so many possibilities for wide acclaim and coveted prestige. As the coach of the Dallas Cyclones, Grady would have all the secretarial help he deserved, to say nothing of a salary that would take him to the very top of the ladder.

"Grady, I'm just so happy for you," she said with an irrepressible smile. "Not that you haven't earned it, but—"

"Let's not rush things," he cut in. "They still haven't offered me anything in writing, so when they come into town next week to see me—"

Now it was her turn to interrupt. "They're coming here to talk to you about it? Oh, Grady, that means that they've got more than just talking on their minds! Of course, they'll probably want to discuss salary and—"

"No doubt about that," he agreed with a disparaging laugh. "I know all about the bait they use from my past experience with them. It can be powerful stuff, Lorna, even for someone like me. If I'm not careful, I'm liable to find myself being auctioned off like a prize cut of beef."

Suddenly, Lorna had the uneasy sense that they were not speaking the same language. Or if they were, Grady was viewing the whole situation from a perspective that made no sense to her. "Well, there's a more positive way to look at it," she pointed out earnestly. "The fact is that they've got the money to offer to the right person, and when they find him, they won't have to hold anything back." She could not keep from smiling and was so pleased by this new prospect that she had to refrain from hugging him. "Oh, Grady, it's a wonderful opportunity, don't you see? I'm just so proud of you! And when they come to see you next week, it won't hurt to make an extra nice impression. I think you should definitely wear your new suit. When they see you in it, they'll probably want to offer you at least a million dollars just to keep you interested!"

She paused when she realized that he was scrutinizing her as coldly as if she were a total stranger. What had she said to provoke this response? But of course! In her enthusiasm, she might have gone a little too far, and she hastily sought to make amends. "I know you don't like to get dressed up, Grady," she said with a soft smile. "In this case, though, you might want to make an exception. There are certain rules that people sometimes have to observe for the sake of success and—"

"Wait a minute, Lorna." He had been sitting on his desk, but now he rose, an imposing figure with his towering height and hair so red that it was the most brilliant source of color in the room. "We obviously have different ideas of success, you and me. Mine doesn't include jumping for the biggest dollar even when it's offered. The fact is that I might not want the job. I might want to stay right here in Larksborough, the closest place to paradise that I've yet found in this world. And I have to know whether you could accept that decision, Lorna, before we go on any further." His eyes bored through her so deeply that once again she felt naked, exposed. "You owe me the truth. So tell it to me. Is that decision something that you could live with, or would it bother you like a thorn in your side every time you were with me?"

Oh, he wanted to know too much, far more than she could easily explain. Why couldn't he just leave well enough alone for the moment? Things often worked out for the best, after all, without being subjected to such brutal amounts of honesty. Lorna closed her eyes. She did not want to lose him. How could she want to lose the man she loved? And yet because she loved him, surely she owed him the truth. At least that, always that.

She forced herself to meet his eyes. "Yes, Grady, I—I think it would bother me. But only because I care for you. I'd want you to have the things in life you deserve, and if you turned your back on them, I'd feel you were cheating yourself." She drew a painful breath, not wanting to go on but knowing that she must. "I suppose I'd feel that you were cheating me, too. When all is said and done, Grady, a certain way of life is important to me. I—I just can't pretend that it isn't."

If honesty was the best policy, then it was one that found no reward in this situation. For a long, awful moment, Grady said nothing, but simply assessed her with narrowed eyes. His face was cold, guarding, it seemed, some raw anguish too terrible to be revealed. "You know what you've told me, don't you, Lorna? You've just told me good-by."

She stood up on shaky legs, her heart beating

like a caged bird within her breast. "Grady, no!" she implored him. "That's not what I meant. Please try to be reasonable. We can work things out; I know we can!"

"How?" he retorted bitterly. "With your needling me every time you see me about how I should wear the right kinds of clothes? And about how I should act and think and talk and breathe?" He shook his head, even as he laughed without joy, the sharp edges of his laughter wounding her heart like a weapon. It was a cutting sound, but it was also a lament, the saddest she had ever heard. "I thought that I could make you see things my way, Lorna. I wanted that so much. But you don't even know who I am, do you?" For a split second, he seemed about to move in her direction as if to shake her or perhaps to take her in his arms. Lorna could not tell. Then he thought better of it and stayed where he was.

"I want you to do me a favor," he told her, his whole body tensed as if to keep from shattering. "I want you to leave now. Please, Lorna. Just get out of my sight before I lose control!"

"Grady, I—"

"Leave! You've already said good-by. There's nothing more that you can say or do."

The room spun before her eyes, even as she dared to catch a glimpse of his face, hard with fury, its bold lines set with absolute decisiveness. No, at that moment, she did not know him, for he had become a stranger to her, still beloved but fully unfathomable and beyond all of her powers of understanding. This, then, really was good-by, except that she could not bring herself to say it. Instead, she slipped soundlessly out of the room, and although her willowy form had vanished from it, she knew she had left her heart behind.

Chapter Ten

There were, Lorna discovered, days when you could not trust yourself to dress, present yourself to the world and perform your job in any kind of rational manner. The day after Grady's birthday was such a day for her. She did not try to fight it but succumbed to the need to stay at home where she could deal with her grief in a private way. The only outside contact she dared to make was in the form of a brief telephone call to Roger Haskell's secretary during which she mumbled something about being ill.

Yes, she was sick, but she couldn't share her problem with Roger's grimly efficient secretary. She was sick at heart, and as her long, empty day wore on, she found that her ailment brought her far more misery than any physical illness that she had ever known. Grady was gone from her life with the warmth and laughter that were as Irish as his name. Perhaps it was inevitable that she had lost him as she had; surely this was the only possible end to a love affair that had never been meant to last. These bitter reflections, though, only brought her further grief. How much better if she had never become involved with him at all, for her journey with Night Train, although filled with moments of joy and gladness along the way, had only carried her to a destination where she knew she could not stay.

How could he have really expected her to condone a decision to stay in Larksborough, she wondered bitterly as salty tears ran into the corners of her mouth. While other people moved ahead in order to claim the prizes and the rewards that the world had to offer, Grady McGraw, it seemed, would be content to remain in one place for the rest of his life, going backward instead of forward, not even caring that everyone else quickly passed him by. Well, let him break all the rules in such a senseless, stubborn way, but not with Lorna Lambert at his side! She would never understand such behavior, nor could she ever sit back quietly and pretend not to mind when he turned his back on every symbol that stood for success. Yes, she loved him, but love was not enough when two people were as vastly different as they. And although she knew that she had lost him fairly, even honestly, that knowledge brought her precious little comfort. There were no simple misunderstandings between them that could be waved away, only a wall so grim and implacable that surely it would keep them apart for the rest of their lives.

She was, however, not the first woman to suffer from the unpredictable ways of love, nor would she be the last. When the next day came, she was ready to go to work as usual, almost looking forward to it as an escape from her personal anguish. The only thing that made her feel apprehensive was the possibility of seeing Grady at the office, although it was more than likely that she would not. He visited the *Courier* infrequently those days for the sole purpose of depositing the weekly articles he wrote in Roger Haskell's mailbox. There was little enough cordiality or even mutual respect between the two men, and Grady preferred to keep his contact with Roger at a minimum. If she saw him, Lorna surmised, it would only be for a fleeting second, possibly in a hallway where they would nod to one another and then go their separate ways. Yes, such encounters would be painful, but they would be so brief and impersonal that Lorna supposed that she could stand them.

Thankfully, however, she did not see Grady at all when she returned to work that day, although she discovered that a grave turn of events had taken place in her absence.

"What's wrong with everyone around here?" she asked Madge Perry, the plump food and feature writer who occupied the desk across from hers. Everyone in the office, it seemed, wore a long face that day, while Madge, who had just returned from the ladies' room, looked for all the world as though she had been crying.

"We've just lost Billy Ray Turner, that's all," she explained with a dab at her reddened eyes. "He had a terrible run-in yesterday with Roger, and it looks like he's going to be leaving us for good."

For a moment, Lorna could not believe her ears. Billy Ray couldn't leave the *Courier;* he had spent his entire career there, and no one knew the people and politics of Larksborough better than he did. How could the newspaper possibly manage without him? The expression on Madge Perry's face, however, assured Lorna that Billy Ray was leaving, although for what reason she could not even begin to imagine.

"But why, Madge?" she persisted, still numbed by a cold sense of shock.

"According to what Roger says, it's because Billy Ray doesn't have a college degree and refuses to go to night school to get one," Madge explained bitterly. "That's only half of the story, of course. Roger never liked Billy Ray from the beginning, and everyone knows it. He's just been looking for a way to get rid of him, so this is every bit as good an excuse as he needs. It's the rottenest thing I've ever heard of, but Roger won't change his mind. Neither will Billy Ray, I'm afraid." She shook her head sadly and gestured to Billy Ray's office. "He's still there if you want to say good-by to him. But you'd better hurry. He just came in today to pack up his personal belongings, so he won't be here much longer."

Lorna took off in a flash, and when she reached Billy Ray's office, her unpleasant shock began to give way to an even unpleasanter sense of reality. It was true; Billy Ray really was leaving, for the once-cluttered walls of his office were now as barren as the surface of his desk. He was, in fact, placing his coffee mug and a framed slogan that read, "The faster I go the behinder I get," inside a cardboard box. He looked pale and shrunken, far from his usual chipper self.

"I guess you've heard the news by now," he told Lorna gravely. "Well, not everybody gets a gold watch after thirty years; not always a handshake, either. That's the way things go sometimes, so try not to look so downhearted. Fact is, I never set much store by gold watches, anyway." He made an attempt to shrug philosophically, but he could not mask the signs of turmoil and deeply wounded pride that haunted his face. "I can't even say I'm too surprised," he mumbled as he looked about the office for anything that still needed to be packed. "I felt it coming for a long time, but to tell you the truth, I just never thought it would come quite like this!"

"Billy Ray, have you thought over the alternatives?" Lorna heard herself say in a desperate attempt to stop him. Then she bit her lip suddenly, wishing that she had never asked such a question. Roger had clearly given Billy Ray no alternative other than the humiliating one of enrolling, at the age of fifty-three and with thirty years of newspaper experience, in a beginner's course in college journalism.

"I'm not a schoolboy any longer." Billy Ray chuckled disparagingly. "I'm too old and opinionated to be the teacher's pet, and even if I managed to get all A's on my report card, I can't see that it would amount to much more than a hill of beans. I've been doing my job here for thirty years. If Haskell doesn't like the way I do it, then sending me to school isn't going to change his mind. Let's face it, Lorna. I'm an old-timer, and my time is finally up." He lifted one of three boxes, all of them containing the odds and ends of his career at the *Courier*, and balanced it in his arms. "So I'll just clear out now and carry all of this stuff to my car."

"Please let me help you," Lorna offered quickly as she picked up a second box. Soon she and Billy Ray were on their way to the parking lot, joined in this leave-taking by Smitty Cummings, one of the other reporters on the staff. They made a solemn and unsmiling trio as they loaded the boxes into Billy Ray's car. At the moment, there were no words that anyone could utter to improve the situation, so they said nothing, working quietly until they were finally finished.

"Billy Ray, what—what are you going to do now?" Lorna asked him softly after he had slammed shut the trunk of his car. She almost didn't want to hear the answer. At fifty-three, it would not be easy for Billy Ray Turner to find another job, and as far as Lorna knew, his salary at the *Courier* had been his only source of income.

"Don't worry about it, Lorna," he said, trying

to reassure her with a pat on her shoulder. "My wife Martha still has her job at the post office, so we should be able to get along just fine. I don't know," he added with a final shrug. "Maybe I'll be able to get in some fishing." Sudden tears moistened his eyes before he reached out to her in a heartfelt hug. "You take care of yourself, you hear? You've got your whole young life ahead of you, so there's no reason for you to worry about a tough old coot like me. I'll manage. I always have, and it's a sure thing that I always will."

Then he was off in his car, leaving the *Courier* behind for the unchartered new life that lay ahead of him. And if his departure from the newspaper where he had worked for thirty years was abrupt and unceremonious, it certainly seemed fitting enough under the circumstances, Lorna concluded bitterly. It was, after all, the Roger Haskells of the world who lay down the rules for people like Billy Ray to follow. If they didn't toe the line, then they were banished from grace, cast out to fend for themselves. Never mind that it was harsh and unjust punishment. It was exactly that, but it was also, at the same time, simply the way things were. As Lorna watched Billy Ray drive off, she experienced a sense of injustice that nearly made her tremble. This feeling was a facet of life that she had never seen before, one so painful that she wondered for a moment if she could dismiss it from her mind in a soothing effort to forget that it had ever happened. But no, she could never do that. Billy Ray was her friend; she knew that she must help him in any way that she could.

The following day, she and Smitty Cummings drew up a petition that protested the manner in which Billy Ray Turner had lost his job. Although the other reporters all signed it, none of them expressed much faith that it would serve the desired purpose of causing Roger Haskell to rehire Billy Ray. "Haskell is the boss's son," Wayne Dykes, the photographer, reminded Lorna with a cynical smile. "And if I know him like I think I do, this petition won't bother him a bit. Oh, he'll give it the once over, and then he'll just toss it into his circular file along with his daily junk mail. He's the one who runs things around here, and he's not about to let us peasants tell him how to do it."

As bleak as Wayne Dykes believed the situation to be, he did not object to taking the petition with him to the football practice at Southern Tech to obtain Grady McGraw's signature. Grady was sure to sign it, Lorna knew, and when he did, it would show that all of Billy Ray's friends and coworkers stood behind him one hundred percent.

She was not disappointed. When the petition was returned to her, she was deeply pleased to see Grady's signature at the bottom, a dark, boldly written scrawl that conveyed a forceful sense of anger. "I've never seen him so mad before," Wayne Dykes told her confidentially. "He was about ready to explode when I told him what had happened. Of course, with that red hair of his, he can look something fierce. For a moment there, I was afraid that he'd burst right into flame."

Lorna's heart wrenched alarmingly at those words. Although she knew that seeing Grady would be difficult, she had never realized that merely hearing of him would be so painful. It was, though, especially in this case, for such a lively description brought back memories that she wanted only to forget. Who knew better than she of Grady McGraw's capacity for full-blown anger? And who knew better than she of his store of tenderness, which was just as passionate and just as filled with vibrant life? Yes, she knew both sides of Grady so well that even a brief description of him had the power to flood her mind with images as sweet as they were bitter. That, though, was the price that she must pay for falling in love with a man who was so wrong for her. Lorna squared her shoulders as she carried the petition to Roger's office. How odd to think that while she and Grady stood together on Billy Ray's behalf, they were miles apart on nearly everything else that mattered!

Roger, however, reviewed the petition very much as Wayne Dykes had predicted. True, he did not throw it into his wastebasket, but he showed no signs that he would let it influence him, either.

"I'm sorry if you feel that Billy Ray was treated unfairly," he told Lorna, his handsome face as smooth and unruffled as ever before. "You must remember, though, that he left his job of his own free will. I assure you that the *Courier* would have been happy to pay for his education, but he refused that opportunity, most ungraciously, too, I might add. So you see, I gave him every chance to stay, but he was simply unwilling to abide by my rules."

"Yes, but perhaps the rules could be adjusted in this case," Lorna said, trying hard not to let her growing anger make her sound irrational. "Billy Ray gave thirty years of his life to the *Courier,* so the issue isn't whether or not he can do the job. It's one of hurt pride on his part and—"

"That's hardly the point," Roger cut in, belittling her remarks with a wave of his hand. "You must realize that the *Courier* is a business enterprise and not a charitable institution. As the managing editor, I cannot afford to concern myself with the peculiarities and foibles of each of my employees. I must lay down certain standards, and if these are not met by a particular individual, then he simply does not belong on my staff." Roger laced his well-manicured fingers together and smiled from behind the polished expanse of his mahogany desk, his poise fully intact. "Surely, you can understand my position, Lorna. I'm not out to win a popularity contest but simply to run the *Courier* as I see best."

How utterly futile, then, the petition had been, Lorna thought stormily as she left Roger's office. All of the signatures in the world would not change his mind, including the angry one of Grady McGraw. It was Roger who was in charge of things, and all of Grady's wrath, as imposing as it might be, would do nothing to change that grim fact. Grady was as powerless to help Billy Ray as was the rest of the staff. They were peasants, all of them, at the mercy of the high and mighty Roger

Haskell! How could she ever have found him attractive at all, Lorna asked herself accusingly. Underneath his elegant and impeccable façade, there was not a decent bone in his body!

Although he had earned the hearty dislike of every one of his staff reporters, it was apparent to Lorna that business at the *Courier* would continue in very much its usual way. Yes, the others still grumbled about Roger. They occasionally lamented the loss of Billy Ray Turner, too, but as the days went by, they mentioned him less and less. It was almost as though he had never been there at all, for in the crunch of daily pressures, more immediate and exciting issues invariably intervened.

One of them, of course, was the final football game of the season, promising, as it did, the league championship for the hard-playing Rebels. It was all that the other reporters seemed to think about, and when it was discovered that the Dallas Cyclones were actually considering Grady McGraw for a coaching job, talk of football dominated the office completely. "I'm putting all of my money on McGraw," Wayne Dykes said with hearty confidence. "Now that the eyes of Texas are upon him, he's got too much at stake to let me down. I say he'll win this big one just like he's won every other game all season long!"

While Lorna could not help but be interested in the outcome of the game, she viewed it from a far different perspective than did Wayne Dykes. For one thing, she knew more than he did, although she kept her information quietly to herself. If

Grady did lead his team to victory, it would not be due to a desire to coach the Dallas Cyclones, she reminded herself. He had all but told her that he would turn down such a golden opportunity, and the thought of it still sickened her. How could he throw his life away so rashly? Besides, the incessant talk of football at the office was starting to upset her. Didn't anyone remember Billy Ray Turner, or was he just an old man who had been pushed aside and forgotten?

Nevertheless, and for whatever personal reason he might have had, Grady McGraw did indeed lead the Rebels to a thoroughly satisfying and highly charged victory on Saturday. All of Larksborough went wild, for the winning of the championship represented a matter of personal glory to nearly everyone in town. Blue and yellow banners flew jubilantly on front lawns, while in the business district, the Rebels' victory became the cause for a gleeful celebration that lasted for several days. Grady McGraw, it seemed, had sparked more excitement in Larksborough than it had ever seen in the course of its quiet history. As the result, he was catapulted to the ranks of a conquering hero.

The *Courier* featured his picture prominently on the front page, including a variety of lengthy articles on him as well. Some of them explored the highlights of his playing career, while others examined his coaching strategies in minute detail. And throughout these reams of copy ran the question that was now foremost in nearly everyone's mind: how long could Larksborough claim him as its own before he was lured to Texas for bigger and better things?

Lorna dismissed such speculations with a cynical eye, because she alone knew his real intentions. Let the others say what they would, she told herself grimly. Grady would soon speak for himself to the amazement of everyone in town but her. When Wednesday came, she quickly ruffled through the pages of the *Courier* to find his weekly column. Surely he would make a statement about his future plans that day, and she was anxious to read it with her own two eyes.

She found, however, no such thing. To her utter astonishment, Grady did not even mention his new job offer; instead, he devoted his entire column to Billy Ray Turner. Not only did Grady devote words of praise to Billy Ray's career, but also he expressed outrage at the manner in which he lost his job. He concluded by roundly condemning the tactics of Roger Haskell. "If I handled the players of my team the way the management of the *Courier* handles its employees," he wrote, "then I wouldn't have achieved one victory all season long. Loyalty is what makes a successful team in sports and in every other walk of life as well. Because I believe this so strongly, I cannot lend my support to the management of the *Courier* any longer. As a result, this will be the last column that I write for the paper. It is the only way that I can call attention to the treatment leveled at Billy Ray Turner, and I'm confident that my readers will understand. I hope, too, they will share my views and that they will come to his defense by making the management of the *Courier* fully aware of how they feel."

The readers did just that, and in no uncertain terms. Shortly after Grady's column appeared in print, the newspaper office was deluged with telephone calls, all of them from readers who angrily wished to cancel their subscriptions to the *Larksborough Courier.* The telephones continued to ring incessantly all day and well into the next, so that extra operators were called in to work the switchboard. The situation had grown to emergency proportions. By Thursday afternoon, it was alarmingly clear to everyone that the *Courier* had lost a full third of its subscribers. "Things don't look too good for the lord of the manor," commented Wayne Dykes, who had recently made a visit to Roger's office. "He's got a peasant uprising on his hands, and he's just fit to be tied."

Which was precisely what he deserved, Lorna concluded before she dismissed a fleeting picture of Roger, red-faced and sputtering, from her thoughts completely. She could only think about Grady now; his spirit made its presence known in every fiber of her being. She had bid the man good-by only a week before, and frantically she tried to remember why she had done so. It had something to do with his not meeting her high standards in life, but in light of what had just taken place, whose values were the ones in question? Certainly not his, for he was the most valiant man she had ever known, one whose sheer strength and kindness nearly made her want to run to him and place her head at his feet. And yet she had been fool enough to believe that he was somehow not worthy of her. The thought of it made her face burn crimson with shame. Oh, how blind she had been to turn away from the splendid gift of his love when he had offered it to her. Surely she would never find another love as golden for the rest of her days.

So great was her sense of remorse that it caused her to witness the events that followed with the dazed eye of a sleepwalker. Roger's father, who owned the newspaper and who had been away on business, was called into town to handle the crisis. This he accomplished behind the closed door of his son's office, emerging at last to make a carefully worded announcement. Roger, it seemed, having gained two years of valuable managerial experience in Larksborough, would be immediately transferred to a recently acquired Haskell family enterprise in Dallas. Billy Ray Turner, on the other hand, would return to the *Courier* in the role of its new managing editor. "I believe that this arrangement will be beneficial to all parties concerned," Grover Haskell explained hastily before he departed for Dallas with a tight-lipped and thoroughly subdued Roger at his side.

It was the best and most satisfying ending, Lorna thought gratefully, for everyone except for her. Perhaps, though, she did not deserve the happiness she longed for, not when she had revealed herself to the man she loved as a shallow and empty-headed fool.

Why, until now, had she been unable to see him for what he truly was? She had merely judged him from the surface, trying all the while to fit him into some slick version of twentieth-century knighthood, complete with blow-dried hair, tailored suits of European design and an aura of elite elegance. But he would never fit such an image. His rust-colored hair was far too unruly to be tamed, while the boldly irregular features of his face would never qualify him as being handsome in a traditional way.

Weren't these, though, part of the very reason why she loved him? Neither his body nor his spirit could be tamed; nor could they ever be made to conform to a prefabricated image. He was simply himself, Grady McGraw, a unique, larger-than-life man who was unlike any other she had ever known. Like the Allegheny Mountains that rose to the west of Larksborough, there was a grandeur about him, and a warmth, too, that came from the core of his heart, radiating outward in life-giving rays that touched everyone who crossed his path. Yes, he was a knight, after all, a far more shining one than she had ever seen in glossy photographs. And yet she had turned away from him!

Perhaps she should run to him now and ask for his forgiveness but she was afraid that he might not want her back. How many chances did one get with a man like Grady McGraw? Besides, even if she swore a thousand times over that she was ready to share his kind of life, why should he believe her? She had, after all, done nothing but try to change him from the day of their first meeting. Somehow she knew that she must bring him proof that she loved him as he really was. But what kind of proof could she offer him, and where would she find it?

Chapter Eleven

"Billy Ray, wait!" Lorna grabbed her coat and breathlessly dashed down a hallway in the *Courier* building to join the paper's new managing editor. "I'm on my way to the press conference, too," she told him, "so why don't we go together? If you'll just give me a few seconds to tidy my hair—"

"No time for that." Billy Ray chuckled, obviously amused by the unusually disheveled appearance of his conscientious fashion writer. It was a windy day, and she had recently returned to the office from an assignment, looking harried and blown about. "The conference is starting in just ten minutes, so we'd better hurry." He placed an arm companionably about her slender shoulders and began to lead her outside. "You can fix yourself up in my car if you want to," he advised her. Although he had been elevated to the rank of managing editor, Billy Ray did not fail to keep touch with daily events and happenings. As a result, his newsman's eye was as keen and zesty as ever before. "And watch your coat, why don't you? You're buttoning it up the wrong way."

So she was, she realized; it was just one more sign of the helter-skelter state of mind that she was in. Not that it really mattered. She had far more important things to cope with now. Yes, she was out of breath and flustered, but she would make it to the press conference in any way that she could.

Soon she and Billy Ray were driving in his car to the Bellcrest Hotel where the conference would be held. Lorna made a hasty attempt to pat her hair into place, trying all the while to calm her nerves and to prepare herself for the momentous risk that she was about to take.

Not that anyone else was aware of how much she personally had at stake. As far as avid football fans and media people were concerned, the much-heralded press conference would be a very public news event where Grady McGraw, triumphant after a winning season with the Rebels, would officially announce his decision to move on as head coach of the Dallas Cyclones. True, he had not yet said anything to indicate that he would accept the Cyclones' offer, but no one, it seemed, who knew the first thing about the sports world seriously doubted that he would do otherwise. How could he, after all, when the Cyclones had doubled their original offer of the week before, now luring him with a salary that amounted to a king's ransom? Top-flight coaches did not remain for long in college football, as people in the know were pointing out. Once they had proved their merit, they invariably blazed ahead to the pros where the sky was the limit and the rewards were as spectacular as fireworks.

"Let's face it," Billy Ray remarked as he parked his car near the Bellcrest Hotel in downtown Larksborough. "Money talks, even to a guy with as big a heart as Night Train McGraw. I'll sure hate to see that man go, but I can't really say that I'll blame him. He deserves another shot at the big time. Besides, he's got nothing to keep him here, no permanent ties or family connections. I guess we should just count ourselves lucky that we had the chance to rub shoulders with him for as long as we did."

Lorna had to shut her eyes against a gathering sense of foreboding. Maybe Billy Ray was right. It was possible that Grady had been destined to enter all of their lives for only the briefest period of time before he finally departed for another world, another place. Certainly, there was nothing to anchor him in Larksborough permanently; only his rustic piece of property on Paradise Lake where he had made his home for the past two years. Lorna tried to breathe deeply and evenly as she walked inside the hotel lobby. Now that winter was approaching, the view from Paradise Lake would be stark and beautiful, but with the arrival of spring, it would become softly green as tender leaves opened themselves to a delicate wash of sunlight. In whatever season, though, it would be a place of wondrous tranquillity where two people could share their lives with each other in time to the peaceful beating of their hearts. And what more could anyone wish for, unless, of course, the promise of dazzling lights from a distant city became too tempting to ignore?

The excitement generated by the press conference was something that Larksborough's venerable Bellcrest Hotel, which dated from the stagecoach era, had never seen before, nor was it likely to witness again. Its largest meeting room overflowed with visitors. Lorna recognized some of them as curious townspeople, but others, those with sophisticated cameras and flashbulb equipment, had come from points throughout the nation to cover the important event for the TV stations, news services and sports magazines that employed them.

One of them, in fact, with the unmistakable good looks and polish of a TV anchorman, had already begun to interview local citizens for their reactions to Grady McGraw's soon-to-be-announced decision.

"Well, we're appreciative of everything he's done for us here," explained an elderly local resident who was approached with a microphone. "But we don't own him, so we're trying to be good sports about it. The way I see it is that Larksborough's loss evens out to be Dallas's gain," he concluded generously. This was greeted by a spatter of applause throughout the room and a general spirit of consensus. No, McGraw had not yet issued his statement, but there was little doubt as to what it would be.

Lorna searched the faces of the crowd frantically. None of them, though, belonged to the person she so desperately wanted to see. He was, it seemed, waiting until it was exactly four o'clock before he entered the room. Lorna checked her wrist watch anxiously. That was only five short minutes away. Then he would take his place at the long table that had been set up at the head of the room and make his official announcement to the members of the press and media.

Five minutes was not a long time, but to Lorna it was an eternity. In five minutes, it might be too late. She had to see him now. With her heart in her mouth, she pressed past the crowd, making her way to the head of the room. Beyond it was a door that led to a hallway. Surely he must be waiting out there, she thought boldly, and surely she would find him.

The hallway, however, was being vigilantly guarded by several hotel attendants who stood in front of the closed door to still another room.

"Look, miss, we have instructions not to let anyone through here," one of them told her testily, as though he had been bothered all day long by pushy hordes of people. "Coach McGraw will be out in a few moments to make his announcement, so you'll have to go back and wait with the others."

Lorna, though, charged by a sense of single-minded determination that seemed to spring from sheer nerve alone, could not stop, not when the rest of her life hung in such precarious balance. She ignored the attendant altogether and darted past him with lightning speed. Before she knew it, she had entered a small waiting room.

Yes, he was there, she saw with relief as she

leaned briefly against the door to steady her trembling body. He was sitting on top of a desk, an achingly familiar figure that also looked for some odd reason like someone she had never seen before. He was surrounded on all sides by a group of men who seemed intent on giving him advice. One of them was Jarrett P. Reynolds, whom Lorna recognized as a prominent local attorney. He held a calculator in his hand and was now sharing the results of his computations with Grady, a gleam of triumph in his eyes.

"No matter how you figure it, McGraw, the Cyclones are giving you one hell of a deal. You'll live like a king on the basis of those stock options alone."

Grady said nothing, although he studied the calculator thoughtfully, his head bent in concentration. Then he raised his eyes to notice the sight of his unexpected visitor, who was still standing breathlessly against the door. His face seemed to register little except for an unwelcome sense of surprise.

"It should be clear that I don't need another opinion," he remarked coldly, "especially when I already know what yours will be."

She moved toward him, scarcely aware that her legs were actually carrying her forward. It was a moment so intense that peripheral details lost all meaning for her. Time and place no longer mattered, and if the other men were watching her curiously, she did not even notice them. There was only Grady, whose challenging blue-green eyes drew her like a magnet. Just Grady alone and the words that she had come to say.

She stopped on shaky legs when she was close enough to touch him. He wore, she realized for the first time, the navy blue pin-striped suit that she had chosen for him, and it was this that made him look so different. He almost looked like a stranger to her! A cold wave of panic engulfed her. He was not the same as she remembered him; for a terrible moment, she felt sure that he had changed completely. But the unruly cowlick that had grown back to appear stubbornly at the top of his head offered her a glorious sign of reassurance. She smiled at him gladly. Why had she ever thought that she had fallen in love with this man? She had not done that; she had risen to love instead, so that she was able to stand before him now in a radiant state of grace and with a heart so filled with feeling that surely it had the power to transform the world just as surely as it had transformed her.

"I do have an opinion, Grady, but it isn't what you think," she told him softly, her eyes never leaving his. "I think you should stay right here where you have a little piece of paradise waiting for you. That's something that all the money in the world could never buy."

His face seemed to open to her even as his eyes bored through her relentlessly, searching, she knew, for signs of flippancy, even deceit. Finding nothing of the kind, he rose to his feet and took her wrist in his hand. "Come on," he told her urgently. "We're getting out of here."

He led her with impatient strides out to the corridor where he waved away the still-watchful attendants. The two of them were alone at last to face each other directly, while a hundred unanswered questions hung suspended in the air.

"So you've had a change of heart, Lorna," Grady began quietly, his generous mouth slipping into a slow smile. "You don't even look the same. You've got your coat on crooked, and your hair looks like it's been attacked by an egg beater." Nevertheless, he did not seem to mind, for he began to stroke the silken, errant strands of her hair into place with tender fingers. "Tell me now, what happened to the old Lorna whom I once knew so well?"

"She—she learned a few things about what really matters in this world," Lorna whispered in a tremulous voice. "Things like loyalty and friendship, and most of all, love. She was awfully lucky because—well, because she had a marvelous teacher." He rewarded her with a look so warm and overflowing that it intoxicated her like champagne. "Oh, Grady, you just can't leave Larksborough for Dallas," she blurted out imploringly. "It would never be right for you, no matter how tempting it might seem at the moment."

"It doesn't really tempt me all that much. The only thing that ever made me think twice was the thought that even paradise might get lonesome from time to time."

She swayed toward him without even knowing it. "Yes, but—but you wouldn't have to live there all by yourself. I mean, I could—you could—" She stopped herself suddenly. Her feelings for him had made her bold, but she had not become so brazen that she could now speak what was foremost in her heart and soul.

"Oh, Lorna." She felt his arms about her, pulling her close to the hard, muscular strength of his body that even now carried the fresh, bracing scent of the out-of-doors. "I may not be the most conventional man in the world, but you'll have to let me say the next words. I love you. I love you so much that I don't want to have to live my life without you." His voice grew husky with emotion, and he drew a long, ragged breath before he continued. "I want you to marry me, Lorna. I guess you know what that means by now. I don't offer a lot of razzle-dazzle, but I can promise to give my lady enough love to keep her warm for the rest of her life."

Her voice caught on a sob. "Oh" was all that she could say.

"Now how am I suppose to take that?" he asked as his lips trailed hungry kisses on her hair, her cheeks and her forehead. "It could mean yes, but it could also mean no."

"No! I mean it doesn't mean no, Grady," she corrected herself in a rush. "It means yes, yes from the bottom of my heart. I will marry you. And I'll love you for the rest of my life."

Then he kissed her so passionately on her lips that she felt herself grow weightless, almost as though she had been transformed into a fluid substance that was now melting against him. Nor had she any doubt that he would keep his promise to her. He was igniting her already with a heat so intense that surely it would burn forever in her veins.

At last, he drew away, and Lorna, resting her

head on the smooth fabric of his suit, heard herself laugh softly.

"I know I'm a funny guy," he said, grinning, "but I hope you're not laughing off my proposal of marriage. I was never more serious about anything in my life."

"Yes, Grady, I know, but—" She succumbed to a joyful peal of laughter. "Why are you wearing that suit? I almost didn't recognize you in it."

"Well, it's grown on me, you might say," he drawled with a devilish chuckle. "I never really had anything against it, but I did want to make my point with you. And now that I have, I thought I might save it for special occasions. Actually, I thought you'd kind of like that."

"Oh, I do, of course, except that—" She bit her lip. It was wonderfully becoming on him and all, but she realized that it was his rumpled old look that was far more beloved to her. "Just as long as you don't wear it too often, Grady. I don't want you to change for me. Please, stay just as you are."

"I'm planning on it," he said, grinning. Then he took her hand and began to lead her into the meeting room where the members of the press and media were eagerly awaiting to hear his official announcement. "Let's go and break the news to all those people in there. They're bound to be surprised when they hear how little I've really changed, so I'll want you by my side. Besides, you better get used to it. You'll be with me for a long time to come."

As they walked hand in hand into the noisy

meeting room, Lorna's eyes avidly drank in every detail of his form, his face and his head of arrestingly red hair. What more glorious way could she live the rest of her life than by standing at his side? There had been a destination promised to her, after all. With the man she loved she had found her own paradise on earth.